© 2023 Joshua Lange

Joshua Lange
With God We Burn

Published by: Cinnabar Moth Publishing LLC
Santa Fe, New Mexico

Cover Design by: Ira Geneve

ISBN-13: 978-1-953971-97-5

Library of Congress Control Number: 2023944152

With God We Burn

JOSHUA LANGE

Thanks for your support!

Best wishes,

Josh

7/21/24

Jo L

Chapter 1
June, 1096 – Constantinople

With my hands clasped and my eyes closed, I prayed. Lord, please protect my father and I. Bless us so that we might get by – even if it's only for a few more months. Please, lift our spirits and ease our burdens. I squeezed my eyes shut tighter, pushed my knees firmly into the cold floor, and sat up straighter, as if that would somehow hasten my communication with heaven. I want to travel to Jerusalem. I want to complete my pilgrimage. Please, dear God, allow this to happen. Allow us to find our way to your holy city.

My next thoughts had been my heaviest, and I hesitated in sharing them with God, even though He already knew. Father says I should be content. He says I should simply wait until a path to Jerusalem opens. But it doesn't feel like it's that simple. Please, guide me, Lord… Amen.

I gazed up at the impossibly high ceiling, which was marked with delicate, colorful paintings of Jesus, and a clear window that was like a view to heaven itself. The dusk sunlight beamed down upon the hundreds of loyal church followers and cast many of us in a deep, orange light.

The church was supported by stunning pillars and walls made of stone and marble, and featured stained glass windows that depicted the miracle that was the life of Jesus. They showed him bearing the crown of thorns, suffering on the cross, healing the sick, and returning to life – they were all a reminder that our pain was nothing in the grand scheme of things. A person-sized crucifix watched over me from the far end of the room.

I concluded my prayers feeling energized but unsatisfied. I didn't allow my impatience to get the best of me, though, especially inside this house of salvation. I darted by the Greek citizens in their brightly colored dalmatic tunics and headed outside.

The city had been truly unbelievable. A far cry from France, where things were held together mainly by wood and farmland. Here, the Greeks had a towering fortress surrounded by stone walls and towers, compact and circular. The buildings were largely tall and secure, like ever-watchful stone trees. It was packed with citizens along the bustling main street.

The Greeks visited shopping stalls and restaurants, bought new clothing and loudly made trades. Even after being there for a year, Constantinople had remained truly foreign to me. The noise of shopkeepers hailing potential customers and the nearly blindingly bright colors of clothing in yellows, blues, and purples were enough to distract me on my way home.

It was hard not to get absorbed in the beauty of the city, but truly, I had been an outsider to Byzantium, and as part of the Catholic Church, it hadn't exactly been the warmest welcome for my father and I. Even now, I remember the hostile glares and turned up noses from the purple-wearing nobles. I remember looking down at my own unassuming, tan tunic, picking at it, feeling how ragged it was, and most of all, how inferior I'd felt.

The Great Schism between our two faiths was still fresh in memory. In the time I'd spent inside their churches, I'd kept to myself, and held all of my prayers within.

I looked left up the long main street, all the way up, at the gigantic, unreal palace in the distance. It was a stone marvel, twice the size of any castle I'd seen back home. It was situated on a large hill, so it towered over us, with its own massive tower that likely allowed seeing miles. The Byzantine emperor, Alexios, was marching up the twisting stairway leading to the palace. He was followed by an armored group of his soldiers. Damn nobles, I thought. And damn Greeks. They all look down on me, and on father. I can't stand it.

As I reflect, I have been unfair to Alexios. He would prove to be important in my life. More than that, he was the leader of the Eastern Christians – our brothers and sisters in faith – and he would become an ally to France. And I have been unfair to the Greeks, too.

I continued down the main street, where the full, beautiful breadth of Constantinople's biggest church shone. Its gigantic dome and four pillars extended up towards the sky like spears, with gorgeous paintings of priests on the side wall, and one of Christ on the dome itself. It had always been a heartening sight. Soon, I refocused and headed towards home.

Further along the main thoroughfare, there was something of a town center, where thousands more gathered. They chatted, played, and enjoyed life. Nearby, many others cheered on horse races that were taking place on the extensive round track. There, several lavishly dressed nobles placed their bets on the potential winners.

I turned a corner near a popular restaurant, and the smell of good food made my stomach growl. I hurried down a small street to my abode. As I got close, I felt the heat from the forge, and heard my father as he hammered away. I dashed inside the house to see if I could grab some food.

Father had already set dinner on the table. It smelled good, though nothing like the fancy restaurant. It was a small beef stew, and an even smaller serving of bread. I gobbled down a few bites.

I scurried back towards the front door, and I nearly tripped over the supplies of wood and charcoal we'd gathered for the forge. I nearly slammed into father on my way out. He grabbed me before we crashed into each other.

"Easy there, Julien. What's the hurry?"

"Hello, Father. I just wanted to get something to eat, but I didn't want to keep you waiting."

"Yes, well, you are late. You should get home earlier tomorrow. You wouldn't want the Greeks finding out you're a Catholic, would you?"

"Sorry, Father."

"It's all right. Come on out and help me finish up."

I nodded, and we continued outside. Father was finishing a fine sword. It had come through on one of our few recent contracts. The bare, steel blade was laid out across the sizzling-hot anvil. Father handed me a pair of thick leather gloves. I put them on, and then he tossed me a hammer. It almost dragged me down to the ground as I caught it. He chuckled, while I grumbled.

"My arms are tired," Father said. "Give it a few good hits, all right?"

"Okay." I lined myself up and gripped the far end of the sword, leaned down to check its evenness, and then gave the sword a good thwack. I paused, and gave it another. After a few more, I got a good rhythm, and evened out our newest creation.

4

"Well done." Father brought over the guard, and together we set it on the bottom of the blade. He'd already measured the grip, but I helped him attach that, and then I hammered it down until it was firmly secured. With that, he displayed the blade, turned and twisted it, and it reflected in the orange light from the forge and the fading sun. Then, he handed me the blade. It was heavy, and it strained my muscles to keep it in the air. But truthfully, it was easier than it had been a few months ago.

Father looked at me intently. "You're becoming a man, Julien."

"Huh?" I laid the completed sword on a nearby table, which also featured several other weapons we'd completed, from a mace to a flail and spear, but they were mostly swords.

Father said, "You've gotten bigger. Your muscles are growing from helping me at the forge." He folded his arms, with his big leather gloves sticking out on the sides. "Your legs are in good shape, too, from our long trek to get here. Unlike mine." He grinned.

I sensed that my father wanted to press me on something. It was a question he had asked me many times before, a question I was afraid to confront. Instead, I drifted away into the house before he could ask.

Dinner was quiet. Father and I sat opposite each other, and I crunched away on the beef and vegetables. When I was finished, I was still hungry. My eyes passed over the third chair at the table. That one would remain empty. Then, I gazed outside the door as the sun disappeared below the horizon. It welcomed a twilight sky, a stunning full moon, and a chillier evening.

With the plates empty, slowly but surely, my mind wandered.

"Father... when can we leave the city? When can we go to Jerusalem?"

"When it's time. You and I will both know when it's right."

"You've been saying that for months and months."

I felt a tension rise between my father and I, like the heat from the forge had wafted into our home and taken up residence. Father tapped his fingers on the table, softly at first, but then more firmly and quickly.

"And you, son, have been ignoring my pleas for as much time."

"What?" I cried.

"You've got a thick skull, my boy. I think you're spending too much time at the church, and not enough time on your sword work."

I stood and pressed my hands on the table. "I'm giving too much to God – is that what you're saying?"

Father stood as well. I heard his bones creak and crack. "Prayer is well and good. But sometimes God asks us to take action. You need to take pride in being a man and realize that you've been called."

"So you're saying God would have me march out on my own and fight my way to Jerusalem?"

"Don't insult me." Father smacked me across the cheek. I recoiled. "I'm saying you need to prepare yourself for war, because it's coming. You've been fooled by the Greeks' colorful games. The Muslims have to answer for what they've done. They ripped the holy land away from us, and they're doing Lord knows what to the faithful people there." He paused. "Julien... God needs men like us to deliver that answer."

Even back then, I didn't understand what my father meant. I had heard of the Turks. They had different beliefs than us. But they were people too. They were part of God's creation. Yet the only knowledge I had was my father's vitriol, and faint whispers from distant Greeks in passing.

Regardless, the path to Jerusalem was blocked, according to my father.

My body shivered. Aside from my doubts, the possibility of battle made me dizzy and uneasy.

Father looked at the empty chair at our table. It was slightly pulled back, as if keeping it that way would allow my mother to return from heaven to join us. Father turned his stern eyes to me.

"What would Len think? Would she be proud of you – trembling, weak, and incapable, like her was when she was ill? Or would she want a son who would protect her, and her faith?" He reached across the table and grabbed me as I pulled away. Emotion welled up inside of me.

I shook my father off and raced outside the house, and my tears streamed behind me. I ran and ran, bumped into confused citizens, and nearly tripped more than once, until I ran out of energy. I breathed with my hands on my knees, with tears that fell to the dirt below, and then slowly raised my head.

I was at the docks. There were dozens of ships, some small for fishing, and some gigantic for battle. Byzantine soldiers equipped with swords, maces, bows and shields were being ferried over the water to the other side – to the east. Other guards patrolled the shore. As for me, I felt more and more alone, and staring across the Bosporus towards the unknown hadn't helped.

That's where it is, I thought. The pilgrim's path to Jerusalem. As the cool breeze caressed my hot, swollen face, I took a long, troubled breath. I resented what my father had said, but in a strange way, I knew he was only looking out for me. It was a deadly question: what if? What if I had no choice but to fight? What if the Greeks were invaded, and I was forced to help them?

I tried to confront new possibilities – and my fear – in my mind. I had pictures of adventure. I swam across the water, stormed onto the beach, and raced off into the dark on a horse. In the back of my mind, I wondered what it would be like to face a Turk in battle. I remember the naïve image I had created of them in my ill-informed youth – they were hazy, dark shadows wielding black swords.

As another patrol of guards headed my way, the nerves struck me, and I dipped away into a darkened area behind some crates of fish. The nautical smell was overwhelming, but it was still better than being caught. I listened in closely as the guards spoke.

"Did you hear about the letter?" one asked his nearby ally. Their boots were heavy in the dirt, so the words were a little hard to hear from this distance.

"What letter?" came a confused response.

"Apparently, the emperor reached out to the west for help."

"What? But… that can't be possible."

"No?" The man pointed out to the moonlit water. "That ferry was the third to leave tonight. We have the weapons to fight, but we're running out of men. The Seljuks are pushing us back at every turn… I'm worried about Constantinople."

"The Muslims would never break through here. Never. This fortress would not fall."

"I know. But the rumor is, the response from Pope Urban was friendly, even hopeful. Supposedly, he's gathering a force to aid us. He wants to capture Jerusalem."

"I'll believe that when I see it." The patrol circled back around, and murmured uncertainties every step of the way.

I pressed a hand on my chest as my heart raced. The pope was important to me, second only to God. He was the figure with the closest connection between heaven and earth. The mighty, infallible bridge between the two realms. Even hearing his name had given me shivers. But could this news be just that – a rumor? Either way, it was one thing for my father to summon me into an army – but if the pope himself had asked, that was different. My mind spun.

I brushed my stray tears away, and with no guards nearby, I stepped out near the water. I stared out into the dark. After a while, I calmed down enough to head home.

By now, the main street was lit by a long, impressive line of torches. The crowds had died down, and the shops were much quieter. I passed by a few, and one building in particular caught my interest. Here, the fish actually smelled so good that my mouth watered. I peeked inside, only to meet eyes immediately with the shopkeeper, a young woman in a bright green dress. She smiled slightly, before she carried a smoky, sizzling dish over to possibly her last customer for the evening. I was tempted to leave, but my eyes were locked on the food.

"What are you up to over there?" she asked, and my attention snapped back to her.

"Oh, I was just passing by." I feigned a smile of my own, and took a step back.

"Did anyone ever tell you you're a bad liar?" She chuckled, and I frowned. She glanced at her customer, then back to me. "Are you hungry?"

"No, I…" I paused. "I don't have the money to eat here."

She waved me over. Hesitantly, I stepped inside. I sat down at a free table and looked around anxiously. There were several other tables, all lit by candles, with another door in back that likely led to the kitchen. The woman's customer, an older man with a big belly, stared at me before chowing down on his food. The lady returned with another plate. This one featured a smaller fish. She set it down in front of me.

"Listen," she said, "my husband runs this place, but he's traveling. I'm filling in for him. He wouldn't like that I'm doing this, but go ahead. Eat something."

"Really?" I stammered. "But why?"

"You look a little thin. Boys need their nourishment." She paused, and a frown set in on her face. "My son... he didn't make it to your age. How old are you?"

"I'm fifteen, ma'am. I'm turning sixteen this summer. Um... do you mind if I ask what happened to your son?"

"He went out to the battlefield. Out there in the east." She sat beside me. "He wanted to protect me from the Turks."

"I'm sorry..."

"How much do you know about them?"

The question stunned me. I was confronted again with the realization that I knew nothing. I was unable to answer.

She half-smiled. "I've only seen you a few times. You don't seem like you're native to the city. Otherwise, you'd actually know some things." She brought a hand through her long, dark hair. My mind raced with concerns. Is it all right that I'm talking to this woman? She's almost certainly a Christian. The distrust and uncertainty swirled in my thoughts, but it was strange. Right there and then, this woman's care had totally disarmed me. She asked, "Where are you visiting from?"

"Oh, I live here. With my father. We... we came from France." I nodded.

"I see. That's a long journey." My stomach grumbled, and she chuckled. "Go ahead," she added. "Eat up." She pushed her chair back and got up.

I ate the fish in two bites. I sat back and stared up at the wood ceiling. I patted my stomach, totally satisfied. The woman smiled at me, and I found myself embarrassed.

"What's your name?" she said.

"Julien. Julien Allais." I awkwardly waved.

"I'm Maria." She sat down again. The final customer left the store with a half-hearted thank you, and left some coin behind on the wooden countertop. The man took a few steps, stopped, and then turned back. He tossed a few extra coins on the counter. "For the boy," he muttered, before he took off. I was humbled. The lady waved to him and returned her attention to me. "Do you want to know about the Turks?"

I asked myself: Do I? It was such a childish question. Thankfully, I said, "Sure."

"Well, they're Muslims, for one. You know that, don't you?"

"Yes. But... not really what that means."

"It means they are incompatible with Christianity. At least, that's what some of the more extreme elements think around here."

I sat up straight. "Is that why all the fighting is going on?"

"I'm not sure. I don't believe it is, but I wouldn't really be the one to ask. I think it's more about the land. There is a great struggle over territory."

I sighed. "My father asked me if I'd want to join the battle."

Maria glanced down at the table, and tears formed in her eyes. "I couldn't stand to see another boy run off and die." She sniffled and tried to use her hair to disguise her emotion. It hadn't worked too well. "But sometimes, we have to sacrifice for God. Sometimes he asks the impossible of us. My son is in the Lord's arms now. I'm proud of him..." She looked into my eyes. "What do you want to do, Julien?"

I quickly replied, "Faith is everything to me. God is everything."

"Rightly so," Maria replied. "That didn't exactly answer my question, though."

I tensed my fists and felt a fire well up in my stomach. I wanted to tell her the truth in glorious detail: "I want to go to Jerusalem, no matter what. I want to pray in the holiest spot in the world. I want to feel the light of God in that sacred place." But those were not the words that I spoke.

"Sorry, Maria. What I want to do is something I want to keep in my heart. That I want to share with God and family."

"Are we not family, as Christians?"

My head recoiled. I couldn't answer her question, not in the way she had hoped. Politely, I declined to answer again.

"Well, Julien, I wish you well in whatever you pursue." She paused. "In any case, you've had a good lesson for today." She began tidying up. She folded up cloths, and cleared my table for me. "I have to close up shop anyway."

"Oh, okay." I hopped up to my feet and walked to the door. "Thank you, Maria. You were so nice to me. I... I'm not used to that, since I've been here."

"Sometimes it takes a different perspective to truly learn something." Her eyes glimmered with wisdom, but her comment sailed over my fifteen-year-old head. "You should know this, too, Julien: the Lord watches over us all. He will deliver answers even during the darkest days. So have faith, and your answers will become clear." She waved goodbye.

I did the same as I nearly stumbled outside in amazement. I wondered, naively, if I had been tended to by the heavens.

Truly, I had learned an important lesson from Maria, but it was the wrong one. There was a difference between sacrificing for God and being completely blind.

When I turned the corner near my home, my father was waiting for me. He leaned against our home with folded arms. He looked at me, surprised, like he had expected me to still be mad and upset.

Instead, I carried a new hope inside that came from Maria – and from the rumor about the pope. I might as well have beamed like the moonlight and stars above, and I think my father sensed it.

He picked up a wooden training sword, which had been propped up next to him. He tossed it to me, and I fumbled it in my hands before I secured it. He hoisted up another training sword and stared me down.

"You look like you've had a revelation, son," he said with a hint of a smile. "If you'd rather keep it to yourself, that's all right. I just hope you've learned something."

"Yes… I think I have." I tightened my hand around the grip. "But I still have a lot of energy, if you don't mind."

"That's why we're out here. Come and get me." He waved me over with a grin.

"Right." I charged in and tried to smack my father with a good hit, but he dodged easily. He whacked my side, a lot more gently than he could have, and I grimaced. We clashed blades. It was nothing like real swords, where you could hear the metal grind, and maybe even see sparks light up the night. I wondered what it would be like to see that in real life.

We clattered sword on sword for a while longer, and my father corrected my form on more than one occasion, but I managed to land a good hit on his leg. He rubbed it firmly, and then he smiled.

"You're getting better, Julien."

"Thanks."

We headed inside and sat at the table. My father lit a candle and placed it between us. I had to tilt my head slightly to see him.

We worked through a lot of emotion that night. Through my fears, and even more tears from me, I reconciled with my father John. I decided I would train myself for the possibility of battle –

for him, for my mother, and for God.

I would soon find a sign in an unexpected place, but I had no idea how misguided I was.

The summer drifted by. I had a quiet sixteenth birthday with my father, and he had a surprise for me: a new sword to truly call my own. It was bright silver, with a midnight blue guard and grip. I was amazed, and I practiced with it the whole day. I think it had been his way of nudging me ever closer towards the idea of battle, and I had eagerly eaten the bait.

I stopped in to see Maria every so often, which was always a welcome experience. Slowly, but surely, I learned more about the situation in the east. That the Turks continued to press in on Byzantine land, and that Emperor Alexios needed help. But all of that information came through hushed tones and whispers.

It was on one mild summer morning that things began to change. As I entered the world from my deep slumber, I heard many voices from my window. They were scared, confused, and perhaps even intrigued, but I was in too much of a haze to make sense of anything. I shambled out of my bedroll and hurried outside, where my father was.

The main street was packed to the brim. Every Greek must've been out on that day. Yet the street itself was clear. The citizens were backed up against buildings, and they cleared the way like the parting of the Red Sea. I looked towards the emperor's palace. He was headed this way. He led what must've been hundreds of troops, and they were tethered to him with their weapons and shields at the ready.

Alexios passed us by, and his long, flowing black hair trailed behind him. He was tall and thin, with a mighty presence that rivaled his city. His guards marched eagerly behind him, and the imposing group made its way towards the front gates of Constantinople.

"Rest easy, my friends!" The emperor's powerful voice startled me as he called out to Byzantium. "Today, we have allies coming from the west!" I was drawn to his energy. I leaned in to track him as he moved by me. "Together, we are going to stop the Turkish invasion once and for all!" Alexios's last words were distant as he pushed onwards.

My father tapped my shoulder. "You want to go check it out?" he asked. "I'm going to rest. My body aches today."

"But what if the Turks appear?" I cried.

"If a war breaks out, you come find me, all right? I may not love the Greeks, but I trust that the emperor has a strong city, at least."

"Okay. I'll be back soon."

He grinned and gave me a push. I ran after the soldiers along with thousands of other curious citizens. We were a colorful stampede that made the ground rumble beneath my feet. I waved to Maria who watched the scene from her door, and she returned my gesture.

The giant, black gates of the city opened, which let out a long, metallic creak and beamed in more sunlight. I held my hand up to block the glow, and I wove through hundreds of Greeks to pursue Alexios.

He and his forces stepped out into the light, and the gates were closed behind him. I couldn't see a thing from here, so I followed another group of kids up the long staircase that led to the walls of the massive city. Above, there was hardly any room to stand. Countless others were there, and they all peered out into the distance. I maneuvered past as many as I could to get a good vantage point.

The view from here was stunning. Green nature and sun-soaked fields as far as the eye could see. Trees were caught in a gusty wind, and that cool burst flew right up to my face. The city was on the water, but the gates faced away from it. I still saw the Black Sea off to the right. The water glittered on this sunny day, and this new perspective sparked my adventurous thoughts. Who's coming from the west? I wondered. Is there anyone from France? I wonder if I could go outside the gates to meet them...

I reflected on my view from the other side, when I had first arrived about a year ago. Constantinople had looked like a giant monster sprouting out of the sea, and the gates were like its massive jaws. I couldn't imagine how anyone could topple this place.

Alexios and his guards stopped about a hundred feet away from those jaws, under the protective range of the towers. Archers above pulled back their bows and notched their arrows. I heard the strained bowstrings. I didn't notice this detail at the time, but Alexios had called the soon-to-be visitors 'guests,' yet his army had prepared to fight.

In the meantime, the Byzantine soldiers, both outside the city and within, waited patiently with shields held high. Then, a pair of men appeared on the horizon, and raced towards us on horses. They were Byzantine, marked by their armor, and they approached the emperor to relay some news. I couldn't hear what they said. Minutes later, as the anticipation had my body wound up tightly, I thought I heard distant thunder.

And then, the horizon darkened.

It was an army. Thousands upon thousands of people marched towards us. Compared to the Greek forces, whoever was on their way had the emperor beat by an uncountable number. It was absolutely terrifying. In my youthful mind, I immediately worried that these were the Turks. But my fears were quickly allayed. Despite the overwhelming numbers, something was off.

For one thing, many of the soldiers were without weapons. They had few in armor, too. Most were dressed in rags. There were few horses. I could've counted those. Perhaps most puzzlingly of all, there were also women and children among their ranks. As I began to wonder who this mass of humanity really was, they got even closer, and I saw the shimmer of crosses on their clothes.

At the very front of this pack, there was one man in particular who stood out. He had an overgrown beard and was dressed in long, tattered priestly robes. He sat atop a donkey. This single man left the flock, stepped down from his mount, and approached Alexios.

The emperor held up a gauntleted hand, and the man from the west stopped. Alexios raised his shoulders and roared, "What in God's name is this? I asked Pope Urban for a small force – not the largest pilgrimage in history."

"I am Peter," the lead westerner muttered. His voice, strangely enough, exuded authority as well, which is why it traveled so well to my ears. "If you would, consider me a messenger for His Holiness." He paused. "Dare I say, even for the Lord Himself."

"Right. And what do you have to say for yourself, Peter?"

"We will attend to your problem on the way to the holy land." Peter opened his arms wide, and turned to face the massive gathering behind him. He raised his voice higher and said, "And then, we will pry Jerusalem from the hands of the infidel."

An impossibly loud cheer resounded from the people behind him. It sent a shiver through my spine. Are they really going to the holy land? And what in the world is Peter talking about?

Alexios stepped right into Peter's face. He placed a hand firmly on his shoulder. "Listen to me," the Byzantine said. "This army is not prepared to cross the water and face the Turks. You are not equipped for battle. You are equipped to be slaughtered."

"You underestimate us," Peter cried as he pulled away from Alexios. "We will prove you wrong."

The Greek persisted. "Answer this, Peter – does Pope Urban have more forces coming?"

"Yes. A noble army will follow in our stead. But we've no time to waste. Our duty is calling."

"Don't be foolish. Stay behind until the others arrive. You will all be killed if I ferry you over to Anatolia."

Alexios had been reasonable. But Peter called to my heart, where a zealous fire had welled up. I wanted to jump into the crowd and partake in another massive cheer with the pilgrims. This was my chance to leave this city, to continue my journey, and perhaps even to face down the Turks on my pilgrim's path.

Peter declined for a second time, and Alexios issued an order.

"If you want to rush out to your doom, go right ahead. But you will not enter my city in these numbers. I will take you in small groups, one at a time, and ferry you over that way."

A big smiled peeked through Peter's bushy beard. "If that's what it takes. We have no interest in scuffling with our fellows-in-faith."

"At least that is something we can agree on."

Alexios led a small group from this army inside the city, and I hurried back down the stairs to meet them. The city's Greeks were nearly frozen as they watched the display. Meanwhile, I trailed both Alexios and Peter.

"I don't have the resources to feed your army," Alexios noted.

"That's fine," Peter calmly replied. "Whatever you can spare will suffice. For the rest, the Lord will guide us."

"If you say so. For now, I'll get the shops to gather some food.

18

Wait in the town center."

Alexios pushed ahead, and he met with a collection of guards to discuss his plans. The many warriors dispersed. They headed to different shops to gather rations for the western forces, while Peter and his small band knelt and prayed in the middle of the town center.

Everything in Constantinople felt like it had stopped in time, like most of the eyes were on Peter, while the rest observed the massive force left outside the gates. As for me, I was firmly focused on Peter. Eventually, when no fighting broke out, many Greeks went back to business. Their shops, the churches, and the docks. I saw a clear path between myself and Peter, and I decided to take it.

"Hello there!" My nervous words were all but squeaked out.

He opened his eyes. "Ah, hello, young man."

"Sir Peter, right? My name is Julien. Do you... do you come from France?"

"'Sir Peter?'" he replied with a laugh. "You're too kind. Well met, Julien. And yes, many of us do hail from France."

"That's amazing. I used to live there, but my father and I moved here."

"I see. Why have you come to me today, Julien?"

"I want to join you on your pilgrimage with my father. I... I want to join your army."

Peter frowned. "Is that right?" He looked me up and down. "We would hardly ever turn down one of the faithful, but... I must say, I don't see it."

"Don't see what, Sir Peter?"

"The fire. The righteous fire to destroy the enemies of God." He suddenly pierced me with a harsh glare. "I look at you and I see a boy. Your bright blonde hair glows in the sun like the Burning

Bush." He laughed, and I found myself both embarrassed and frustrated. "You would fit in better with the women and children, but I'll tell you that no man among us would allow that. You must be ready to fight." He paused, and studied me again. "You wouldn't make it on the other side of the water. You would be killed." My heart sunk, but strangely enough, Peter might've saved my life. Despite his arrogance, he did leave me with one prophetic piece of advice. "Your destiny may indeed lie to the east, just not now."

By now, a crowd had gathered around the confident Peter. He continued his reckoning.

"People of Byzantium – His Holiness, Pope Urban, delivered a call-to-arms in France. He asked us to free the holy city from the control of the infidel. These people go by many names: Seljuks, Turks, and Saracens. But it is not our duty to know them, it is to destroy them."

I slowly nodded. I was absorbed in his gravity, even after his insult.

"They kill our brothers and sisters here in the east – surely you all know this by now, if you've lived here. But it is worse than that – Jerusalem is under the heel of those Muslim Turks. They blaspheme the holiest sites with their deeds, and their very presence." He paused, and he raised his voice to a boom. "We are the sword of righteousness to smite them." Peter's own passion swelled. His words soon summoned a larger crowd. "My army is here to save the Christian world."

The Greeks didn't seem as convinced of Peter's foolish truth as I was. Many of them had folded arms.

The day concluded as Peter shared his message throughout the city, and I had followed him for much of the way. When I returned home, my father scolded me for being out too late. I told him what happened with Peter, and he was unusually quiet about it. I went to bed that night feeling terribly uneasy.

Despite what the bold, bearded man said, I wanted my father and I to join his armed pilgrimage. It seemed like the only way I would get to Jerusalem.

Chapter 2

When I awoke, my father was kneeling beside my bedroll. He prayed with his crucifix in hand. He opened his eyes just as I looked at him.

"Good morning, Julien."

I half-smiled. "Morning." I sat up on my elbows. "Father... why are you praying here?"

"The pilgrims are being ferried over. Most of them have gone to the east already."

I scrambled to my feet. "Oh, God. We should get ready then, shouldn't we?"

"No. Sit down, son." Father grabbed me, which quelled my frenzy of movement, and then he laid me onto my bedroll.

"What's the matter, Father? Isn't this the answer we've been waiting for?"

"It is for me."

My heart froze.

"My strength is leaving me, Julien. Each week, I feel worse. I have the best chance of going now, while I can still fight. As for you... you're not ready for the journey."

Tears welled in my eyes. "How can you speak so coldly, so callously about this?"

"Because that kind of callousness is what we're faced with. When you set across the water, brutality awaits you. That is what I've been trying to say, son." He looked at me intently as I wept. "These tears make you weak."

I shook my head. "Because I cry at the thought of losing you? "

"You won't lose me, Julien." He touched my arm. "Did you see the army at the gates? We have thousands of men. The Turks won't have a chance."

"Then why can't I come along?"

"Because you weep like a boy. Because you'd be a liability in an ambush." He paused as I stared at him with my mouth agape, and my heart broken. "This isn't the end, son. Peter mentioned another army on the way. Seek them out in my stead. And while you wait, wipe those tears away. Pray deeply. Get stronger."

I avoided his gaze with no words to say. Suddenly, he hugged me, and though I wanted to cry harder, I blocked the tears out. I collected my feelings up into a knot of pure, frozen grief. My father pulled back.

"This isn't just about you and me, Julien. This is about God's will. This all might've aligned for you to find a different path to the holy land, a different destiny. You will have to find your own answers. 'The kingdom of heaven lies within.'"

I smiled. It was a truth that touched me and dried my tears. I made a conscious choice at that moment. To focus on the possibilities instead of the doubts. I wondered about the nobles coming from the west, and where my journey might take me. I mentally drifted away before my father called me back.

"I've given you all the tools, my boy. When the moment is there, follow me." He stood. "I've left you half of my savings. The coin is on the table. You should be all right for a while." I nodded. After hesitating he said, "I'm packed up and ready to go. I'll be on my way." He gave me one last, intent look. "I love you, Julien. I plan on seeing you soon – and when I do, I hope to see you standing tall, and standing proud, as a man and as a champion of the Lord."

"I love you too." I dug deep into my soul and said, "When we next meet, I will be someone that you, mother, and God can be proud of. I will see you in Jerusalem."

"Yes. I'll see you there, son."

We said our goodbyes, and I watched my father walk away. He grabbed a sword on the way out and picked up a big leather bag, which he hoisted over his shoulder. Then, he disappeared into the light.

After a few frantic minutes of second-guessing, I hurried to the docks, and I was able to see the last of the pilgrims ferry over to Anatolia. I waved to them and watched them get smaller and smaller on the horizon. And with that, I was alone.

But truthfully, like my father said, I was never alone. I had the light of heaven within me, and the kindling for the flames of passion. Most of all, I had a goal, the goal of a lifetime.

––––––––––

Over the next few days, I trained. I swung my birthday sword, as well as axes, maces, and everything I had ever forged, as hard as I could. I exhausted myself, and I only took breaks to eat and wash up. I received no work orders at the smithy, but I did accept visitors. First, Maria came to check on me and even offer food.

I'd also made a young Byzantine acquaintance, a guard named Isaac who had taken a liking to me after we'd crafted him a sword. He practiced with me and even taught me some Byzantine tactics, mainly, how to defend and evade, which I had never learned. Day by day, I felt stronger and more confident.

I didn't sleep well, but I prayed each night. I prayed for clarity, I prayed for my father and Peter, and I foolishly prayed for personal strength.

In early September, I may have received another sign from above.

After church one day, I was on my way home, when I saw a priest seated outside the building. His clothes were tattered and ripped in places. The man seemed unkempt, with messy hair and a dirty-looking beard. He reminded me of Peter.

He was in a clump on the ground, and he stared vacantly at the sky. A pile of dusty books rested beside him. The rest of the Byzantine world moved around him and paid him no mind, but I was drawn to him right away.

"Hello," I said. Slowly, his cloudy, dark eyes turned to meet mine. "Are you a priest? Do you mind if I ask what you're doing?"

"A priest?" he asked, and blinked quickly a few times. He looked down at his clothes and patted them softly. "Oh. I was." He glanced down with a frown.

"What do you mean, sir?" I reached out a hand for him. "Actually, can I help you up first?"

"I belong here, but... thank you." Reluctantly, he took my hand, and I dragged him up. He quickly knelt back down to grab the books off the ground.

"Haven't the Byzantines offered to help you?" I looked left and right as the usual bustling crowds passed us by.

"Quite often, yes. But I'd be no help to anyone, so I kindly declined." He paused. "They even offered to have me preach." He half-smiled. "What a joke."

"You're so hard on yourself. Why is that?"

"You have a lot of questions," the man said with a laugh. "I guess I could use a good walk. Want to come along? We can chat a bit."

"All right." I nodded. At that point, I was intrigued. How could someone be a former priest? How could they separate from their connection to the church?

We walked down the main street and bumped into some citizens on our way to the town center. Things were unusually still. Even at sunset, there was typically a lot more activity. We sat under a big tree, which offered us plenty of shade.

"So, what's your name?" the man asked me.

"Julien. And you?"

"Jean. I can tell you're not from around here. Where are you from? Germany?"

"France. And I might say the same of you, Jean. I've never seen you here before." I glanced at him.

"Actually, I'm from France too." He stared off into the distance like he was lost in thought. "I just returned from a pilgrimage in the east."

"You made a pilgrimage?" I turned fully to face him. "What happened?"

"I failed my charges."

I leaned in closer to him.

He sighed emotionally. "I was an abbot. I took twenty of my students with me... I lost them all."

I gasped. "I'm sorry, Jean... Did the Turks attack?"

He turned to me. His eyes had welled with tears. "No. We simply weren't prepared. We ran out of supplies. Early on, I wanted to turn back, but they begged me to push on. They wanted to see the holy land."

I frowned. "I know what that feels like."

Jean studied me. "Are you enduring a trial of your own?"

"Something like that."

We were silent for a while afterwards. I watched the Greeks as they streamed by in their beautiful, colorful outfits. It was like how I'd watch the clouds, calmly and warmly. My feelings on the Byzantines had definitely softened.

Sitting there quietly, it was easy to get lost in my mind. Truly, I didn't want to be here. I wanted to catch up with my father. I wanted to be at the gates of Jerusalem. But this, perhaps, had been a necessary part of my journey. If I had believed anything else, though, it would've been too hard for me to face at that point in my life.

I turned back to Jean. "Do you have a place to go?"

"No," he softly said. "I want to go back home, but I don't have the money or supplies. I'd have to work here for a while."

"You can stay with me."

For the first time, Jean's eyes lit up, and he showed a smile. I could tell that he never expected me to say that. But that smile faded. He said, "Do you trust me, Julien?"

I peered at the former priest. "I couldn't turn away a brother-in-faith."

We headed back to the forge, which had been cold for days now. Jean set his book collection on the table, and I gave him a spare bedroll. Initially, I felt strange letting him stay, like Jean would be taking my father's place somehow, but I let that feeling go with an intentioned, deep breath.

That evening, after asking me for approval, Jean picked up a sword and swung it a few times. It looked easy for him, even natural. I simply watched, and wondered what kind of past this man could've had.

Later, we had leftover stew, and a small serving of bread. Jean ate like it was the first time he ever had food, and it made me smile. I lit a candle as Jean sorted through his books, and he needed more than a minute to brush away all the dust. He plopped down one book in particular and flipped through its pages.

"So what are these?" I asked as I leaned over to try and read the text. The words on the page were unrecognizable. I knew it wasn't Latin, at least.

"Gifts from a friend." Jean spun the book around to help me get a better look. It wasn't any easier to read this way. "He was a Turk. A Seljuk merchant." I glared at Jean. He smiled gently, and added, "I know that must seem hard to believe, but it's the truth."

"So this book is…" I paused. "Their language?"

"Yes. It's called Arabic. More specifically, it's the language of their faith. They use others as well."

I looked at him, shocked, and he grinned. "You have much to learn, Julien."

"What else could you mean?" I grumbled. "This is already too much for me to believe."

"Well, you should know that the Turks aren't the only Muslims. There's another group from Egypt – the Fatimid – and they are warring with the Turks too."

I pondered to myself as I tensed my fists. The unfortunate picture I had painted of the Turks had been clear. I hadn't realized they could actually speak a language, let alone one different than mine. I certainly hadn't imagined there were different factions or other types of Muslims either. Looking back, this had been one of the truly embarrassing moments of my youth.

"Why are you so worked up about this?" Jean asked. "Are you going to war to help the Byzantines?"

"I'm going to Jerusalem," I muttered. "But the Turks have held it hostage. I expect to fight them in the future."

Jean glanced away and narrowed his eyes. "I... hadn't heard that about the holy land." He looked at me and tapped his finger on the book. "Well, if you plan on marching to the east, you should understand what you're getting into."

"What, you mean learn their words?" I was incredulous, with my mouth agape.

"Exactly."

"I don't even know every Latin word, though," I complained. "How am I supposed to learn a second language?"

"You won't – but you should know key things. What if you have to trade in a Turkish city? What if you have to negotiate with their leaders?"

Jean's comments sailed right over my head.

I resisted at first, but Jean helped me start on a new path – one of the mind. Every day, I tried to learn a word or two in both Latin and Arabic – and I think Jean had rediscovered his calling as a teacher. I continued to train and get stronger, and the former abbot even aided me in my swordplay. Eventually, Maria and Isaac connected with Jean too. It was strange. I'd found myself with something of a makeshift family. It was difficult – as I missed my father dearly – but it was beautiful, too.

I endured the month of September, but each day was more challenging than the next. There was no word from the west, and even worse, no word from the east. How had the pilgrims fared? How was my father? When would the next army arrive to fulfill my dream? I had many questions, and no solutions. The pain and doubt drained and overwhelmed me, but I kept my hands together in prayer. I would receive my answers soon – and none of them would be what I expected.

Chapter 3

The month of October came with no sign from the western army. Every day, I walked the walls of Constantinople and looked out on the horizon. I prayed for an army to appear over the hills and summon me into a new life. Each night, I went to the docks and prayed for Father's safe return. Nonetheless, I still took the time to learn and focus on my studies.

Days passed, and it got harder and harder to believe that my dream of visiting Jerusalem would come true. My mind wandered, and I pondered if I should simply ferry to the east alone.

In November, when I was at my most desperate, everything changed.

I awoke to the sounds of Byzantium in wonder and confusion. It was like I had re-lived Peter's arrival. I hurried outside, and Jean trailed after me. Once again, the streets were crowded with people, and Alexios emerged from his palace to walk through the heart of his city. I tailed the emperor, and one of his guards shoved me away because I was too close. Jean heaved behind me, barely keeping up.

I dashed up the stairs to the walls, and I almost knocked several people down as I raced by. I apologized mid-sprint. I found my place and gazed upon the long horizon once more while Jean stood beside me. The emperor settled outside the gates with hundreds of soldiers behind him. All of their weapons were drawn, and the archers atop the towers prepared their arrows.

A collection of Byzantine soldiers appeared in the distance and raced towards their leader in a blur of speed. Like last time, the scouts reported something quietly to Alexios. What followed was another agonizing wait. My heart pounded for minutes.

What I saw next could've been from a dream. The western army appeared, and most of the warriors were in full, knightly armor. They strode with purpose, many on horseback.

The bulk of the knights stopped a fair distance away from the city, but a small group approached Alexios.

"We're here, your Excellency," the lead knight shouted in a high-pitched, boisterous tone. "You must be Alexios. I am Godfrey, and I am here to save you."

Even in my naivety, I thought the man sounded cocky.

Alexios ignored the comment. "Welcome, Sir Godfrey. Is this all of the forces I'll be receiving...?"

"No, not at all. My compatriots are on their way, but they are a little slow as usual." He cackled.

"In any case, I thank you for coming. However... I must set a rule before we proceed." Alexios paused. "I want you to take an oath – I want you to swear that you will work for me on your mission to the east. Particularly, you must give any land you capture back to me."

I saw Godfrey's exasperation from here. "You're serious, aren't you?"

"Extremely." The eastern forces shifted slightly. Godfrey stepped back.

"I'll have to wait for my allies then, Your Excellency." He bowed his head, but his discontent was marked on his face.

This man wasn't at all what I had expected. I wondered if the bright, glowing armor was a trick, a mirage.

Alexios returned to the city with his men, and the gates were slammed shut. The knights, in turn, began construction of a base camp near the Black Sea. They chopped down wood and put up tents. Even I sensed the aggression in this, but I hoped the rest of the western forces would arrive soon to clear the air.

I lingered on the walls, and watched everything these knights did. They practiced swordplay, built up their camp and looked for supplies in nature. Finally, when the sky turned orange, Jean and I headed home. The city was on edge. People spoke in concerned tones, and the town center was totally still.

A few days passed by in a flash, but I observed the knights during every free moment. Alexios did too, understandably so. I had failed to realize the obvious, potential danger of this intimidating army right outside the gates.

The following afternoon, another staggering army arrived. The men who appeared were dressed in darker armor than Godfrey's forces, and they were equally threatening. They were led by two knights, and one was truly a behemoth of a man. He carried an impossibly large sword on his back and towered over even the largest of his allies. His armor was sharp and black, like his vicious sword. Strangely enough, the other leader was a boy. He could've been my age, with short, messy hair and a curious, wicked-looking smile.

Alexios met these new forces at the gates and presented his oath once more. Godfrey avoided the question a second time, while the other leaders simply, and coldly, declined without even introducing themselves. They, too, were shut out of Constantinople. I was split between amazement and confusion. The knights' arrival, and their actions, certainly hadn't gone according to my hopes. Are these really the people that could guide me to Jerusalem? I wondered.

I spent that afternoon trying to guess the number of men in armor. If there are a thousand there, I thought, and a thousand at that camp, and another thousand in the distance... My mind blurred once I approached thirty thousand. Unbelievably, we then got word that a third army was on its way from the west. They wouldn't arrive for several days, according to the scouts. In that delay, I trained, prayed, and watched the knights from the walls.

By that point, two separate base camps had been constructed, and the Byzantines had grown more and more uneasy. I felt the heaviness in the air, and that energy pressed on the shoulders of the city's citizens – myself included.

Then, finally, when the last force arrived, my naïve dreams spiraled away from me.

The last army galloped to the gates with thousands upon thousands of knights in tow, and they had many civilians: priests, women and children. They were led by an older man, grizzled and stern, like he'd seen some hundred wars in his time. He wore full chainmail and a white surcoat, and rode atop a gray horse. I couldn't take my eyes off of him, until I saw his compatriots.

His closest ally was slender, with long, blond hair. He was equally protected by mail armor from chest to toes, and he wore a hopeful smile as he galloped beside the others.

The leaders of all three western armies approached the gates, and Alexios prepared to meet them. As I peeked back inside Constantinople, the emperor had a summoned a group of his soldiers in a circle. I couldn't hear most of what he said, but I did hear one loud remark: "Avoid killing, unless absolutely necessary."

The tension was palpable. The Byzantines beside me on the walls, in the towers, and down below were all wound up and ready to snap. The knights were, too. Many tapped their feet, folded their arms, and worse, aggressively swung their weapons in practice.

I listened in as the knights began to speak.

"Hello there," the youngest one playfully called to the other leaders. None of them responded right away.

"Greetings." the tall blond finally offered. "I'm Bishop Adhemar, from France. And Sir Raymond is with me." He pointed to the older knight, who hopped off of his horse. The other leaders followed suit.

"It's good to meet you all," the boy said. "I'm Tancred, and I fight beside my uncle, Bohemond. We hail from Italy."

The massive man bowed his head. "Welcome. I see your forces rival our own." His calm tone wasn't what I expected from the giant.

"Lastly—" Tancred was cut off by the knight who, even back then, I had been ready to call pompous.

"Godfrey, yes. We're familiar with each other, don't you worry." He grinned. "I beat you again, Raymond. I got here first."

Raymond sighed. "Good for you. Anyway, why are you camped outside like this?"

"Alexios is holding us up."

"I see. With this many soldiers, I suppose he's worried a fight could break out."

"Yes, but food is dwindling. The men are getting uneasy."

"I can tell. What's the latest news?"

"Alexios had the nerve to ask us to pledge our loyalty to him." Godfrey lowered his voice. I couldn't hear what he said next.

Raymond laughed. "'Making a move?' What, you mean raiding our allies?" The response prompted more Byzantine soldiers to gather atop the walls. Isaac sprinted past me and took up a position nearby with a bow in hand.

I was shocked. I couldn't understand how the knights could've threatened their friends-in-faith. It hadn't seemed like it was because of the Great Schism.

Godfrey faced out towards Raymond's forces. He muttered, "It's either that or risk starvation. I'm sure we all used up plenty of supplies on the trek here. Regardless, your men don't seem eager to sit and wait, either."

"That may be," Raymond maintained, "but I don't agree with your plan. I want to hear what Alexios has to say about that pledge." Raymond raised his head and stared at the entrance to Constantinople. I was thankful that he seemed to have some sense.

That said, both men had remarkable confidence. At any point, the Byzantines could send a flurry of arrows their way.

I heard a loud clank. The gates were opened. Alexios led hundreds of guards out to meet the westerners. The guards' swords, spears, maces and shields reflected the sun's light. They ended their approach about a hundred feet away from the knights, grouped up in a defensive formation, with their shields held high. Alexios drew his blade. The knights responded. Some of the men in the camps grabbed weapons of their own, and the forces behind Raymond stirred. My heart pounded.

"You're all that's coming, I would hope," Alexios sternly said. "I asked Pope Urban for a small force to aid me. First, I received the largest pilgrimage in history. And now, I received possibly the largest army on earth. What am I to do with that?"

"Help guide us to victory," Godfrey blurted out. "You know

36

what we're here for, Alexios. Why can't you simply let us do it?"

"I explained this already. Take the oath. Then you can cross over to Anatolia."

"Excuse me," Raymond said. "I've just arrived from France with Sir Adhemar. I've only now heard of this oath. What do you wish of us?"

"When I turn you loose on the Seljuks," Alexios continued, "I want to be assured that you're going to give any land taken from them directly to me. Everything they own was mine before. This is my home. I can't have westerners rolling in to slaughter everyone and take the Turks' place."

"How dare you," Raymond suddenly shouted. "You think we would turn our army against you?"

"The impatience in your men is apparent. 'Making a move,' wasn't it? My men have ears, you know. You've been rather callous in your displays thus far."

Raymond groaned, but he was left without words. We all knew what Godfrey had just threatened to do, even if Raymond had laughed it off.

"I have to protect my city," the emperor said. "Think of the burden if I let thousands of hungry people march inside. What do you think will happen? You knights must pledge that you'll work for me – then we'll talk. Then you'll be fed."

The leaders from the west were silent. I focused on Raymond, who was squeezing his gauntleted hands into fists.

"We marched here to help you," he growled, "to save you from the Turks. Yet you want us to kneel at your feet?"

"We both know that's not the goal of your army," Alexios replied. "The forces that came here before you – they are the proof of that. They were a fanatical group of peasants set on besieging Jerusalem." My head recoiled. How could Alexios say that? I wondered. Peter came here to help him, and my father went to war, too. Alexios added, "Each of you is going to have to prove that you're better than that. Prove that you have the discipline and honor to cooperate with me."

"You're a pompous fool," Godfrey said. "You're not in control here. Our godly army could push your city right into the sea if we wished."

"Go ahead and try. You'll find yourselves dead before you see a single Turk."

Raymond's frustration continued to build. I felt it emanate from him, and waft in the air like heat from the forge. Bohemond and Tancred remained quiet, though the giant had reached around to touch the sword on his back. It was Adhemar who stepped up next.

"Gentleman, is there no room for discussion here? We're tired. We've had a long trip. Can we send groups into the city – say, a hundred at a time – for meals? Could we start there while we negotiate?"

"I must insist on the oath," Alexios maintained. "I'm sorry. This isn't the way I want it – but it's the way it must be for the safety of Byzantium."

"Men, to me," Godfrey shrieked. He summoned men from one of the camps, and they rushed out in droves to his side. "I'm sick of this. We'll do things the hard way, then."

"If that's your choice, then so be it."

My heart dropped, and I felt sick. Were the faithful truly going to come to blows? Was there no other way to resolve this? And why did these men only seem to think of battle?

Hundreds of soldiers unsheathed their weapons. My ears rang as the metal scraped, and the noise echoed.

There was a standoff where things fell eerily quiet. My heart continued to race with anxious beats.

It was Godfrey who made the first move. He and his men moved ahead and clashed with Alexios's forces. They smashed swords and maces into the defenders' shields, but the formation held against the first attack. Godfrey himself locked swords with Alexios and they struggled for control.

With the battle's eruption, warriors from the rear began to press forward. The sounds of battle had sent a spark throughout the western army.

Raymond lunged ahead next, and a contingent of his men followed after him.

I remember the Byzantines being unperturbed, unafraid, as they deflected sword strikes and locked metal against metal. I couldn't believe the first skirmish I'd seen was between Catholics and Christians.

With a heavy strike, Raymond disarmed a guard and knocked the shield free from his hands. He had an opportunity to follow up, to wound, but he didn't. He let him pick the shield up from the ground. I took a nervous breath and surveyed the rest of the battle.

It seemed that Raymond's hesitation was echoed throughout this skirmish. I saw no blood, no wounded, and I was thankful for that. Godfrey fought against Alexios, but I might've said that he flailed instead.

Adhemar was off on his own. He pushed back multiple guards by himself. Tancred held his own, too, as he violently battered several guards with his blade. Bohemond, to my surprise, had opted not to use his sword. Instead, he used fists to grab and smash enemies into the ground. The giant deflected maces with his black gauntlets and punched aside shields to get to his targets.

I was heartbroken. This wasn't right. Why was this happening?

The western army seemed to have things well in-hand. However, I noticed the rear army had encroached closer, and threatened to join the battle. The numbers were already uneven. The west outnumbered Alexios's forces five-to-one. If the rest of them joined, the emperor would have no chance, and this battle would likely turn bloody.

Raymond pulled back after another quick strike against Alexios. "Stay back, men," he boomed. "We'll be inside the city shortly."

After emotional minutes passed, things had become more even. The defenders remained in a tight formation. They were unbroken by the western advances. The Greeks were calm, and I noticed that the western leaders had gotten tired. With my tactical view, I saw that Raymond especially had trouble catching his breath. As the exhibition continued, the tides fully turned. Even though the west had the numbers advantage against Alexios, he and his men stayed strong. The defenders seemed almost as impenetrable as their city.

The knight leaders had to give up. It was that, or risk embarrassment. They would've soon swung their heavy weapons with tired arms like they were underwater in the Black Sea.

"Damn it," Raymond shouted. "We yield, Alexios."

"Thank you," Alexios responded with hardly a heavy breath.

"I'm starving," Godfrey muttered. "That's the only reason you won."

"Then you'll take the oath?"

"Yes, yes, let's get on with it. I swear, I will be loyal to you. I bow to you." He muttered something under his breath.

"And the others?"

"I'd already planned to before this madness broke out," Adhemar said. "I will be loyal, Alexios. I promise you that."

Tancred and Bohemond, who had endured the same exhaustion, nodded in unison. Eventually, they muttered their oaths, too. Raymond, however, remained defiant.

"I can't do it. I won't do it."

Alexios stared a hole through him. The knight finally stood down, and he said, "What I can do, though, is promise you something else. I swear upon God – I will never turn against you, never harm your great empire. Is that enough?"

"Your men will eat last, Sir Raymond." Alexios eyed him coldly, and then turned to Adhemar. "As for you, for being the most reasonable, you can join me first. Take a hundred men with you into the city. We'll go from there." He marched back towards his city with his guards in tow.

Godfrey was tempted to chase after them. He took a quick half-step forward, then thought better of it.

After a brief debate about who would join Adhemar, the leaders agreed that Raymond and Godfrey would stay behind as a gesture of goodwill. Alexios would've likely kicked them right back out if they entered first, anyway.

The first group to enter consisted of mostly civilians, picked by the leaders to accompany them. Adhemar took the lead, with Bohemond and Tancred behind him. They made their way to the gates and stepped inside. As for me, I was overwhelmed and emotionally spent by the religious in-fighting. However, I truly believed these knights were the only way for me to get to the holy land. I charged down the stairs to meet them.

Chapter 4

I dashed at full-speed right behind the knights. They actually spun around to face me, but not with open arms. They drew their weapons, and I pulled up short in shock.

"Oh, my God," I screamed as I dropped to my knees in pure fright. "I'm so sorry." I begged forgiveness and clasped my hands together. I realized they must've thought I was going to attack them. I waited, hoping they'd accept the apology, and perhaps even reach out and lift me up, but they didn't. The two Italians actually laughed at me.

"Who is this foolish whelp?" Bohemond said.

Tancred replied, "It doesn't matter, uncle. Let's go." The two of them turned away and headed down the street. Adhemar, though, maintained his gaze on me.

"Why were you in such a hurry, young man?" he asked as he reached out his hand. I smiled and grabbed it. I felt the cold rings of his mail armor against my fingers. Adhemar pulled me up to my feet.

I briefly lost my train of thought. I said, "I'm from the west, too. I've lived here for a while, but... I was waiting for you to arrive."

The knight smiled and titled his head. "And why is that?"

"I want… I want to join your army." I stepped forward.

Adhemar bowed his head. "I think that's a noble idea. I can see your passion, but… I'm not certain we could make use of you. Thank you for sharing your goal with us, in any case." With one more polite bow, he turned and went on his way.

I couldn't have messed that up any more than I did, I thought. I'll have to try again. These people are my best hope.

I trailed the knights on foot while the rest of Byzantium followed with their eyes. I darted from cover to cover, and peeked out from trees and buildings to keep them in sight. The whole city was still. I heard only uncertain, curious whispers. It was one of the most bizarre moments of my life. The city housed tens of thousands of people, and I had never heard it so quiet.

Jean found me on the street and dragged me into some shade. "You've got to settle down," he said. "I appreciate your passion, but stalking them isn't going to help your chances of joining."

"Is that really what it looks like?" I asked, puzzled. Then I realized my heart was pounding like a war drum.

Jean patted his chest a few times. "Slow down and approach them seriously. Show them your faith, just as you did for me." He glanced out at the group of knights, who had continued on to the town center. "They may look like they're a heavenly army, but they are people, just like you and me." He stared at them. "I don't know what kind of people, though…"

"Okay, Jean. Thanks."

For the moment, the two of us returned home. I had to focus my mind, so I decided to start up the forge. Maybe the work would allow me to settle down.

I heated up a blade that I had nearly finished before father left.

I placed it atop the anvil and hammered away. With each crack of tool on steel, I envisioned my goals. I want to continue my journey, I thought with one. I want to pray at the holy city, right beside my father, came another. Suddenly, I was greeted by some unexpected visitors: Raymond and Adhemar.

I was covered in soot and sweat, and that probably made me look ten years older than I was. Raymond turned to his ally and said, "Is this the 'foolish whelp' Bohemond mentioned?"

Adhemar smiled. "That's him."

I took a deep breath and approached the knights, this time with stern seriousness. Raymond reached out to shake my hand, and I returned the gesture. "So, you have some skills, it seems," he said.

"Only a few," I replied.

"Ahh, and modest too. That is a skill, to be sure, but don't use it too much. You have to assert yourself in life." He chuckled, and I nodded nervously. He added, "We could always use another smith – and perhaps another warrior." He looked at me intently.

Adhemar added, "Yes. It seems I was mistaken in my initial judgment. What's your name, young man?"

I'm not certain how long it took me to respond. In my memories, it feels like it was minutes. I said, "Julien Allais."

Raymond grinned. "Well met. So, Julien, we were told that this smithy was run by somewhat of an outcast. I wondered if you could address what that meant."

"Oh… um…" Had word gotten around that I'm a Catholic? I wondered. But as I looked at these knights, something told me I didn't have to be shy. I said, "I'm not like the other Greeks. I'm a Catholic."

"Well," Raymond said with a laugh, "that makes me like you a little more." He smacked my arm. I couldn't deny the comment was cold and cruel, despite the attempt at humor. But at the time, just like when I met Peter, I was absorbed into the knights' gravity, and into the unity that came from faith, even if it was hollow.

"So what do you want, Julien? Why do you labor in this little corner of a Greek city?"

"I want to go to Jerusalem," I firmly said. "I've been waiting to complete my pilgrimage."

"Well – you know who is in the way, don't you?"

Before I answered, Jean hurried outside. He looked back and forth between the knights and I.

"It seems you got your wish," he said to me.

"Who's this?" Raymond asked. "Your father?"

"Oh, no," I replied. "Just a friend. My father... he went to battle in the east."

"I see." Raymond folded his arms. "Did he join Peter's numbers?"

"Yes," I said as I glanced down. "He left a couple of months ago."

"What stopped you from following him?" Adhemar asked.

I looked at my birthday sword, which rested atop a batch of other weapons. "I had to get stronger. Otherwise, I wouldn't be of use to anyone."

Raymond nodded slowly, and a smile crept across his face. "This must be destiny. With our arrival, you now have a path to your pilgrim's dream. So, Julien – join us. Fight alongside us, for Pope Urban – and for God."

It felt like my whole body had been cleansed with cool water. I was calm, and my spirit was free. As I reflect now, that feeling—that blind certainty—only stirs terrible regret in my heart. I had no idea what Raymond had truly meant, or what I had gotten myself into. But in that moment, nothing else mattered. It was a pure, zealous clarity in my mind.

"I can see the fire in your eyes." Raymond squeezed my shoulder

46

softly, and then stepped back. He looked me over. "You're in good shape, and you obviously have experience with weapons. Do you have any training?"

"Only practice duels with my father, and Jean." I pointed to the abbot. The knights eyed him curiously. They had the same reaction I did when the priest admitted he was a fighter.

"That's a good start," Adhemar noted. "But we will have some time before we ferry over to the east. In the meantime, I'm sure we can train you. Isn't that right?" He motioned to the other knight, who hadn't stopped smiling. Raymond nodded.

"It's settled, then," Adhemar concluded. "Let's get dinner to celebrate." He headed towards main street, followed by Raymond. I turned to Jean with probably the biggest smile I had ever worn. That memory crushes my heart now.

As for the abbot, there was pain hidden behind his warm expression, though I didn't recognize it at the time. I was eager to go on my journey, but I'd have to leave a friend behind.

"Well come on, Jean," I cried, and waved to him as I charged after the knights. "Let's go."

He didn't say anything, but he followed me.

I had recommended Maria's restaurant for good fish, but the knights wanted meat. We stopped at a stall with a sizzling selection to choose from. My mouth watered, but I realized that I didn't have any money to pay. I took a few steps towards home, but Raymond offered to pay for Jean and I.

We chowed down, and my belly was more than satisfied, thanks to Raymond.

After we ate, Jean and I headed back home. We sat at the table and I tried to study a little before the day's end. As soon as I opened a book, I looked up, and Jean stared at me with a frown.

"Jean…" I quietly said. "I just realized – the knights didn't ask you to come along." I paused, and searched my mind for what to do. "I'll go ask them." I kicked my chair back as I got up and almost sprinted out the door. The priest called me back.

"Don't bother. They could sense it, I'm sure – I'm not fit for the journey. And I don't want to go. I already failed my last attempt. I'm sick of Anatolia." He forced a hollow smile. "You should understand something, Julien…" He sat down at the table, and the dim candle light reflected in his eyes. "Anatolia is a brutal place. You'll be marching uphill nearly all the way to Jerusalem, and that's only if you can get past the Turks."

"What are you talking about?" I asked. "We have an army of the faithful. Won't it be easy?"

"You're mistaken." I glared at him. My zealous flames burned. Jean smiled honestly this time. "But I wish you well. I will pray for you, every day."

"Thanks, Jean. What are you going to do?"

"I'll stay here until I make enough money to head back to France."

"All right." I bowed my head in an attempt to mimic the knights. It became another regret on a growing list. "You deserve peace. I hope you find it back home."

"I hope you find it too." He frowned. He looked like he wanted to say something else, but he chose not to.

With that, I headed to bed. The month of November had ended, and my new life was about to begin. I was set to train under the shining knights and prepare for my journey to the east – to save Jerusalem.

Now I would ask: How do you save something that doesn't need to be saved?

Chapter 5

December arrived with only a slight drop in temperature. It had been one of the great parts of life in this city. There was no miserable winter like there had been in France. It was consistent, normal, and expected – sometimes, it made it easy for me to lose track of time. But there and then, I lived in the moment.

Raymond kicked me onto my back for the third time. I struggled to my feet, breathing heavier than I ever had. I tried to smack him with my practice sword, but he avoided every attack like it was nothing. He swung around to my back and tapped me hard with his hilt. I dropped to my knees, exhausted. I somehow managed to stand once more.

"You have courage," the knight remarked as he paced back and forth. "But courage alone won't win you a battle in the east."

"Come now," Adhemar said. He leaned against my house, a lot like my father had months before. It only made me miss him more. The stoic Adhemar added, "You're awfully hard on the boy."

Raymond glared at his ally. "If not me, then who? Should his first trials be against the Turks?"

"Yes... perhaps you're right."

The man's amber eyes met mine. "Try again, Julien. Try to hit me."

I breathed in, and exhaled deeply. I rushed ahead but hesitated with the swing this time. I aimed my blade low, at his armored legs. Raymond allowed me to hit him, and the wood cracked against the mail and splintered into pieces. He hardly budged.

"What are you doing?" he asked me. "You thought that would hurt me?"

I shook my head. "I'm sorry – as we've been practicing, I've been imagining fighting a Turk. I don't know if they have armor like yours, so I went low."

"I see." He tilted his head slightly.

I turned towards the other knight. "Do you know anything about the Turks, Sir Adhemar?"

He pushed himself off the wood and stepped towards me. "I do. I went on a pilgrimage to the east, and I've seen them fight."

I gasped through my tired breathing. "What are they like?"

He cleared this throat, but hesitated in answering.

I used the last of my energy to scurry to Adhemar's side. I took to one knee, and held myself up with my cracked training sword. In the meantime, Raymond took off to collect a meal for us.

The other knight continued, "Pope Urban's description of the Turks would paint the situation in Jerusalem as dire. As if an unimaginable darkness had claimed the holy land. But…"

I'd hardly noticed the knight's words had trailed off into uncertainty. Instead, my mouth had fallen open at the grim description of the holy city. It matched Peter's description almost exactly. However, the tall man narrowed his eyes and thought to himself for a moment.

"My apologies, Julien," he eventually said. "I've just had trouble addressing the… discrepancy… between the views of His

Holiness, and my own personal experience."

I simply stared at the knight, puzzled.

"I've been to the holy city, you know."

Easily distracted by this news, I leaned in excitedly. "What was it like?"

"It was stunning. It has a quality to it that is not of this earth. Though it remains firmly in control of our enemies, it has not lost its wonder."

Raymond returned with a tray of food. He cast a long, intimidating shadow through the alley. He handed each of us a piece of smoking meat, and I ate in a hurry.

"What are you two talking about?" Raymond asked as he set the empty tray down on my weapons table. He took a large bite of his food, and then grabbed a sword to practice with.

"I was telling the young man about Jerusalem and the Turks," Adhemar replied. I awaited his words like a baby waited for a meal. The long-haired knight spoke again, and this time, he spoke the truth. "When I last visited, Jerusalem was safe."

I stood as my breath returned to me. "What...?"

"The Turks let the faithful come and go. They allowed us to pray, and worship freely. And there was no killing or abuse to be found."

Something felt heavy in my mind. I might've called it the weight of truth, of reason, as it pressed down on my naivety and threatened to break it like glass.

Adhemar added, "The Saracens, as we sometimes call them, are intelligent and disciplined. I can still picture the grace with which they rode their horses, the unity of their formations." He paused, and nodded slowly. "But no matter what, I intend to return to defeat them all."

Raymond took two scary-looking swings with his blade. He asked his ally, "You mean to say that something changed since your last visit to the holy city? That the Turks have become evil – but they weren't before?"

Adhemar's face twisted into uncertainty.

"It doesn't matter," Raymond coldly stated. "His Holiness was clear. Our duty is set, and I intend to carry it out."

"I do as well," Adhemar replied. "Make no mistake."

I remained lost, but my heart and soul had sided with Raymond. I wanted things to be easy. I wanted to see the Turks as my mortal enemies. I was wrong – but I had no idea how wrong.

I endured the training with the knights for the rest of the evening. When I was totally spent, night had fallen, and Raymond brought me to the city gates. For the first time since I'd arrived in Constantinople, I stepped outside the walls. The knight brought me to his camp.

I tagged alongside him like a pet, all but latched onto his armor, as I looked up at countless tall, strong, imposing soldiers. We passed by several dozen tents and campfires before we pulled up to a small group of men. I recognized two of them, Tancred and Bohemond, the Italians who had insulted me. Their greeting was cold and abrasive, but once they realized how serious I was, they warmed up to me.

"We'll need to get you some armor, Julien," Raymond said with a smile. The thought perked me up. I pictured myself in huge, shining chainmail, the kind that made me look as big as Bohemond. Raymond added, "You know your way around a blacksmith. Do you make armor?"

"Oh." I snapped out of my fanciful daydreams. "No, sir. I wouldn't be able to do that. I could ask one of the Greek armorers, if you like."

"Ahh, but you're going to be one of us. We'll get you equipped."

Tancred stared at me with a long frown. He narrowed his eyes, and let out a big, heavy sigh. "I might have something that could help."

The knights directed me into one of the tents. Tancred opened a chest, and pulled a few things out. First, a full set of chainmail. The links looked – and sounded – impossibly heavy as the boy heaved them onto the ground. Next, a padded overcoat, a lot like the kind Raymond wore. This one was more my size. The colors were beautiful: deep red and white in four opposing sections. Tancred set it down too, and I admired my new gear. All of it could've been from a dream.

Raymond had an ear-to-ear smile, and he patted my back firmly. I almost toppled over onto the ground.

Tancred glared at him. "I want you to understand something. This was a gift to me from a friend. It's also my backup equipment, in case anything of mine is damaged." He burned Raymond with his eyes, and then focused on me. "I don't want to give this away, especially to a whelp like you. You better prove yourself on the battlefield – or else I'll pry this off your corpse."

My boyish excitement faded as the thought of a real battle entered my mind. I slowly nodded at Tancred. "I promise you," I said, "I will honor this gift. I will respect it. And I will earn it."

"You're full of it," the Italian replied with a laugh. "But I appreciate it."

"May I try it on?" I glanced between the two knights. They both agreed, but then I realized I had no idea how to get the mail on. They showed me. It was as simple as draping it over your body like a shirt. What I couldn't quite anticipate was the heaviness. Every movement was a new sensation, a new strain on a muscle.

The coat slipped on easily and fit perfectly. When I was equipped, I ran my fingers along the mail links. Tancred groaned before he left.

"You look good," Raymond said, "like a real warrior."

"Thank you, sir!" I replied excitedly.

"You'll need a helmet too. We'll get that later." He put a hand on his chin. "And... you'll need a horse, too."

"Are you serious?" I asked, stunned.

"Yes. Alexios has offered many to us. We'll take advantage of it. Do you have training?"

"I learned back in France. I haven't ridden in a couple of years, though."

"Good enough. I'll sort that out, don't worry. Let's head out."

Back outside, I was greeted by the cheers of dozens of knights. They clapped, whistled, and welcomed the new knight-in-training.

I walked with Raymond. We took in the night sky, and the torch-lit camp that bustled around us. I took the opportunity to watch the knight's train. They dueled with swords, raced on horseback, and tried to out-drink each other. Raymond and I came up to a hill that overlooked the Bosporus River. Things were quiet here, peaceful.

"Sir Raymond... I've been wondering something. Why are you doing this for me?"

The knight grinned. "I believe you can help us on our mission." He tapped his chest, over his heart. "I can tell that you have the same passion, the same faith in God that I do." For the first time, Raymond's stern eyes wavered, and he looked at the sky as though he wanted to see to heaven. "That faith will be the most important thing for our journey to the east. We must trust in the Lord, and all else will follow."

I smiled. "Yes, sir."

We observed the water, where the stars cast a brilliant light on the surface. I gazed towards those mysterious, pale white dots and wondered what my future held.

"Sir, if I may ask... will we be ferrying over soon?"

"Not quite yet. We still have to coordinate with Alexios. He plans on bringing us to his palace to go over the battle plans."

"But... wouldn't it be easier if we just left now? We have such a strong army, and my father might've already cleared the way to Jerusalem."

Raymond looked at me intently. "There's more to it than that, Julien."

"What do you mean?"

The knight frowned, and gazed across the water, into the dark unknown. He said, "The Turks are more formidable than you might think. The peasant army failed."

My heart sunk, and my mouth fell open. I grabbed Raymond's arms, and gently, he pushed my hands down. He looked into my eyes, and continued. "While you were training today, the remains of Peter's forces returned to Constantinople. Alexios has them tucked away in the palace."

I tried to run to the palace. I wanted to see my father. Raymond held me back. He took a firm hold of my new surcoat. "Listen," he muttered, "the truth is... if your father made it, he would have come home today."

"No!" I shouted. I drew the attention of dozens of knights. I quietly added, "You can't know that, Sir Raymond. I'm going to the palace."

"If you charge up there now, the guards will turn you away. Alexios is gathering information from the survivors." He breathed in and sighed heavily. "We are going to the palace tomorrow. I'll bring you with me, all right? If your father is there, we will see him."

"I can't wait a whole night," I said as the tears fell.

"You've already waited a long time – just one more night, Julien. And no matter what, soon enough, your dreams will be fulfilled." He smiled slightly and squeezed my shoulder. "We'll go to the holy land, together."

I brushed away my tears, but I could hardly hold my emotion back.

Raymond offered for me to stay in camp overnight, but I declined. I returned inside the city in a hurry. I stared up the long main street towards the palace. It bloomed under the night sky, with candlelight that glinted out of its many windows. I stood there as people passed me by. I waited for my father to step out of the palace doors. But after minutes, and eventually an hour, no sign came. I decided to go home.

On the way, I stopped outside the biggest church in the city, Hagia Sophia. I realized I needed to clear my mind the only way I knew how: prayer.

Chapter 6

I prayed as long as I could, before the church closed.

When I returned home, Jean was stunned by my gear and praised me. I think he sensed my chaotic emotions, and he might've tried to prepare me for my march to the east. But nothing, and no one, could have done that.

The next day, Raymond woke me up early, and we dueled with sword and shield for the entire morning. I was already exhausted, and the sun had barely risen. When we finished, Raymond complimented my progress, but he left me with a grim truth: "I have one last test for you, Julien. Expect it anywhere, and anytime – it is the last trial to prepare you for battle in the east. Keep it in your mind. Be always alert, always on edge."

When the sun had reached its apex, and shined its golden light all across the city, the knight leaders were invited to the palace. I desperately hoped I would see my father there.

I'd never been to the palace, or even close to the twisting staircase that led to the imposing double doors. Godfrey led the way there, with Bohemond and Tancred next, and finally Raymond and I. As if I wasn't tense enough from Raymond's potential test, we were all under heavy guard, surrounded by Byzantine soldiers. They finally dispersed once we reached the doors.

Alexios welcomed us inside, and I was left astonished. The décor was mostly golden, curved and sleek. There were lavish displays of flowers and a large fountain with a stone cross mounted in the middle. A small army of attendants was cleaning, which must have been why everything seemed so shiny and pristine. This had the illusion of being heaven itself, so bright and serene, but even I hadn't been naïve enough to believe that's where we were.

The throne room was dead ahead, and it was an extension of the extravagance. It contained a throne that could've been built in size for a deity. There was a huge round table, with more than enough seats for our group. To the left, there was another large set of double doors. They creaked open.

Peter stepped out, and he could have been a ghost. His confidence, the aura of authority he had once displayed, was gone. He was thin, almost hollow. The man headed towards the exit, trailed by dozens of his loyal followers. The numbers grew until they became a stream of broken faithful. It almost shattered my heart. I desperately scanned the numbers for my father, but I didn't see him. Peter was right on our path. He didn't even look at us as he passed by. I called out to him, and everyone stopped.

The man turned slowly to me. "Oh... is that you, Julien?" He stared at me. "Yes... You've grown. You look like a man now."

"Sir Peter... what happened? Your army... they didn't make it to Jerusalem?"

He glanced away. "It seems the Lord has declined our help." His dark, cold eyes met mine, before he observed the rest of the knights. "Perhaps it is you will succeed in our stead. I will pray for you."

"Have you seen my father?" I cried. "Did he make it...?"

Peter looked at me intently. "Our army split into groups. I don't recall seeing your father. It is... entirely possible that he is out there." He forced a smile. Even back then, I knew it was false.

I barely choked back my tears. "Thank you," I mustered. With that, the defeated remains of the peasant army disappeared out into the sunlight. I never saw them again.

As my hope began to fade, the fires of revenge began to take its place. I tried to shake off those embers in favor of focus – I had to learn about the Turks from the emperor himself.

Our group moved on to the throne room. Here, the men continued inside, but Raymond held out his arm to prevent me from going in.

"What's the matter, sir?" I asked.

"You must wait out here, Julien."

"Why take me so far inside the palace, then?"

"I want you to listen to the discussion – to learn. But you cannot partake. This is for the leaders only. For the men only."

I leaned to the side slightly, and peeked in to see the other leaders. I focused on Tancred. He couldn't have been much older than me. "What about Tancred, though?"

Raymond cleared his throat, and whispered, "I know only a little about the Italians. But I have heard Tancred, like his uncle, is an experienced killer. Tancred knows the ways of war – enough where he can be welcomed inside."

"I think I understand, sir. I'll stay out here." I thought about it. This would certainly be a strategy meeting, and I doubted I would have much to offer. Raymond brought a chair for me, and I sat facing the palace entrance.

"I'm glad you understand," Raymond said. "I'll return soon."

He headed in the join the discussion. I checked the doors. They were kept open.

From here, I listened. I wondered what kind of advice Alexios had prepared about our trip to the other side of the water.

"Gentlemen," Alexios began, "I wanted to first thank you coming to reason – for allowing things to work out peacefully. Our skirmish was regrettable."

"You're welcome," Raymond said. "We had little choice though, didn't we?"

"I suppose. You could've gone to war with me, though, and I appreciate that you didn't."

"Yes, well, I admit that would be a waste. At least we have a common goal to focus on. So, shall we proceed?"

"Yes." He paused. "I've been fending off the Seljuks for months now. You should know what you're going to be dealing with. I would venture to guess most of you have never fought them."

"That's likely true," Adhemar chimed in. "However, I've seen them on my pilgrimage. I've seen their horses, their speed. They use mainly bows, as well."

"Correct. Their main strategy involves horse archers. They'll attempt to surround you, to slay you before you get close." Everyone was quiet. "You saw our defensive formation earlier – it acts as a counter to their tactics. You must draw their attention, hold out, and flank them. Use your cavalry. I believe you outnumber them by thousands. Your chances of winning are strong."

"Thank you," Raymond said. "We appreciate the guidance."

My mind raced with images of how our battles would play out. In my naivety, I saw overwhelming success. Now, those images are stained blood red.

"Indeed," Bohemond added. "I can't imagine you brought us

60

out here simply for a strategy lesson, though."

"You're more quick-witted than I expected," the emperor replied. "But yes, you're right. I also think you should be aware of the way the Muslims think. Their goals... their ideology."

"Pope Urban had a lot to say about this," Adhemar said. "He called them unholy. If I may... before your advice, Alexios, I'd be curious what everyone here thinks about that."

"His Holiness is exactly right," Godfrey barked. "The Turks are destined to be routed by the righteous. That's what we're here to do."

I reflected on Jean's words, how he had befriended a Turk, and Sir Adhemar's hopeful description of Jerusalem – could it really be as simple as Godfrey made it sound?

"As far as we're concerned," Tancred responded, "they are God's enemies. We came here to wipe them out."

"Exactly," Bohemond muttered. "It's either that, or we die and go right to heaven. In both cases, I'm content. But make no mistake, I'll kill a hundred of them for any warrior we lose."

"Hear hear!" Tancred's words echoed around the huge throne room.

"I agree with His Holiness," Raymond began. "I believe that we must free Jerusalem to allow this world to find peace. The Saracens, Seljuks, whatever we want to call them – they are an unholy army, and that is why they had the strength to push you back to your capital. That's why you summoned us, wasn't it, Alexios?"

"No, it wasn't," the emperor grumbled. "I wished for a small group to contain them."

"You really are pompous, aren't you?" Godfrey groaned. "We're here to save you – without us, you would be doomed."

I heard a loud crack – possibly the emperor smashing his hands on the table. Whatever it was startled me. "One more word,"

Alexios said, "and I'll have you thrown in the Black Sea."

The tension may as well have wafted from the room. I was tempted to look inside, but I stayed put. Thankfully, Adhemar spoke up. "We're all on the same side. Let us work together – as Sir Raymond said, we have a common goal. We are all believers in the Lord, soldiers of God – is that not enough?"

After a long moment, there was a unified response from the westerners: "Aye."

Alexios cleared this throat. "I have one last piece of advice – you would do well to respect the Turks. I've spent a lot of time fighting them. I'd like to say we've earned each other's respect. I disagree with what's been said thus far – the Turks are believers in their own faith, much like you, and in my eyes, they are fighting with the same fire."

"What?" Godfrey shrieked. "How in God's name can you say that?"

"Because I've seen it for myself. They may be wrong – completely and utterly so – but they believe it just the same."

"What does that mean for us, Alexios?" Raymond asked.

"It means that when you push them, when you strike them with the passion of God, they will have to strike back twice as hard. Look at their perspective – you're marching out to destroy them all. With this army of yours… you'll not receive any kindness from the Muslims. And respectfully, you shouldn't."

Even back then, I knew the emperor was right.

"Hear hear," Raymond eventually said. "Though I'll be honest – I don't think any of us here were planning to be merciful."

The room fell quiet as the leaders contemplated. As for me, I was torn between the desire to rush across the water, and my unease about my allies. Alexios broke the silence and pulled me out of my mind.

"Gentleman, I have a request. The Turks have a general – a man called Elchanes. He has given me a great deal of trouble over the last few months."

"Go on," Raymond said.

"He's the right hand of the Turks' leader, Kilij Arslan." He paused. "Not only has he been a thorn in my side, but he also led a massacre of your people – the peasants – at the castle garrison, Xerigordos."

I quietly gasped.

"What?" Godfrey shrieked. "Are you certain?"

"Yes. Your people tried to capture it, but they were routed and destroyed, save for a few survivors. Both Peter and my scouts confirmed this."

"Someone must kill him," Tancred shouted. "Now that we have a name – a general no less – we must avenge the fallen."

I tensed my fists. My first instinct was to agree with Tancred.

"I'll do it," Raymond confirmed. "I'll go to the castle to hunt him – and then I will rejoin the rest of you as you head for the Turks' capital."

"Trying to steal the glory?" Godfrey asked with a cackle.

Raymond sighed deeply. "You get to march right to Nicaea to take on the Turks – you shall have the bulk of the glory. Many of the peasants came from France. I will be the one to avenge them."

"You always did sympathize with the rabble, Raymond. Caring for that boy, Julien, is another foolish example. Well… good for you."

As if my opinion of Godfrey hadn't been low enough, that sealed it. Still, Raymond had done a lot for me so far – it humbled me.

"It's settled then," Alexios said. "When you land on the eastern shore, head west along the coast – you won't miss the castle." He let out a heavy sigh. "If you can bring Elchanes down, that would be helpful indeed."

"Make no mistake," Raymond muttered, "my men will see him dead."

Soon after, Alexios offered us a meal, a proper banquet. His servants walked through the doors, back and forth, and brought round after round of food, with meats, fruits and vegetables each on gold plates. Even in my isolated seat, I tried to enjoy every bite. Before we all left, the leaders had one last question for the emperor. I peeked in.

"Your Grace," Godfrey began. "You don't intend to march with us to Jerusalem?"

"No, I do not. My duty is to my people."

"Don't you see that this is the most important fight of our lifetime?" Raymond asked. "This will affect the entire world."

"I don't mean any disrespect when I say this," Alexios paused, and peered at my mentor coldly, "but that remains to be seen. My duty as emperor remains the same as it always has." The leaders grumbled in frustration. Godfrey was the loudest. Alexios continued, "That said, I plan to help you. I will follow you for a short time and make camp behind you. I'll also offer some of my men."

"Really?" Raymond said. "I do hope that will be enough."

After dinner, Alexios escorted us outside the city to the knights' camps. The sun had dipped deeply and cast a dark orange glow across our army.

"Soon enough," Alexios said, "I'll start ferrying you across to Anatolia. Once you get to the other side... I can't guarantee what awaits you. It could very well be the gates of hell."

The emperor, in this case, was wise indeed.

Chapter 7
Christmas Day

As the twilight illuminated the nearby water and ships, I sat on the dock with my legs over the side. I listened to the water brush against the wood, and I stared out at the Bosporus, that small stretch of water that linked us to our enemies, in an attempt to see beyond the horizon. I couldn't leave yet. The knights still had much to prepare.

It was easy to get lost in my mind. I pictured the battles, the endless possibilities of what my future held. I ran my hands over my face, felt my stubbly beard, and let out a big, anxious yawn.

"Tired, Julien?" Raymond asked, and I jumped. I hadn't heard him approach.

"Oh, um, a little. I've probably been here for too long."

"That's no way to celebrate Christmas."

"I know. I've said all my prayers today. I can't think of anything else to do."

He reached his hand out for mine. "Let's go have dinner. They're doing something bigger at the palace, but why don't we avoid the crowd?"

"I hadn't heard." I grabbed his hand, and he pulled me up to my feet. Without his armor, the knight was a strange sight. He wore a plain tunic, and he looked much smaller because of it. He seemed like an older man now. I noticed his gray beard and hair more easily without the distraction of the shining mail.

"Of course you didn't hear. You were by the water for hours. I had to come find you. I was worried."

"Right… that makes sense."

Raymond moved towards the main street, and I hurried beside him. We waved to some of the dock workers as they stored weapons and food aboard their ships. It was another thing I had been too distracted to notice – the ships were being stocked for war.

"So, what're they doing at the palace?" I asked Raymond.

"It's a big festival. Food, wine, all of that."

"Sounds fun."

"Yes, but we also need time for a little bit of self-reflection. A little quiet time." He glanced at me with a smile. "Though I know you've had plenty of that today."

We skirted by citizens as we continued through the busy streets, and settled on my friend Maria's restaurant for dinner. The smell of fish drifted out through the open doorway. We were welcomed in by the friendly young lady who brought us to a table.

We were the only patrons, so we looked out on a view of the city. People celebrated the birthday of the Lord, and they were lit by the glow of dozens of torches. Families played together. It was a sight that I fully appreciated only later. I didn't want to be in Constantinople. I wanted to be in Anatolia – in Jerusalem – in a battle to rescue my father, who I couldn't let go. I wanted to strike down the mysterious Elchanes. It's something I regret. I wish I had embraced those days in Constantinople.

I sat quietly with Raymond and we both prayed for the future.

When I opened my eyes, Raymond fixed his eyes on me. "Let me ask you something, Julien. Are you going to be ready for this journey to the east?"

"I'm ready." I took a nervous sip of water. "For my father, and for me."

"I want you to understand that this war is going to change you."

I nodded, and swallowed hard.

"We will kill, and we'll do it in cold blood. We'll commit horrors, cruelties, to win this war. That's what we're walking into. That is what God is asking of us."

I set my drink down and leaned in slightly. "How do you know that?"

Raymond smiled coldly. "What do you think will happen when an army of thirty thousand knights marches into a Muslim town? An army that is fueled by religious fire, with a passion that burns brighter than the sun? Think about the people in that town, the women and children, the workers and traders."

It was a dark and bloody picture. Alexios had echoed a similar sentiment – to throw mercy away once we made it across the water. I wanted to fight the Turks. They had delayed my pilgrimage, taken my father away, and harmed the people from France. Still, the notion of being rid of mercy hadn't truly sunk in. "I don't really know what to say."

"Say you'll think on it. Say you'll brace yourself."

"I… I will. Thank you for being honest with me."

"Of course. I know the truth all too well. I've fought in plenty of wars in my time."

We endured an awkward minute while the tension settled, but our host was able to crack through it with a round of wine.

67

After dinner, Raymond walked home with me. There were waves of people hurrying by on the streets, including many knights. Many headed towards the camps, while others marched to the docks.

"What's going on?" I asked Raymond.

"We're going to start ferrying over tomorrow."

I gasped. "Really?"

"Yes. We just found out this evening, before I went to pick you up. This is going to be our last restful night, I suspect, so... I wanted you to enjoy it."

"Thank you, sir." I was touched by his kindness. "All right, I'll get my things together. I don't have much, anyway."

"Will you join us at camp?"

I thought about it for a moment. "No. I'd like to spend this last night with my friend Jean."

"Okay, Julien. Pray deeply tonight. I'll pick you up tomorrow morning."

"All right. See you then!"

We went our separate ways, and I excitedly ran inside to give Jean the news. He already knew, and he tried in vain to hide his pained expression behind a smile.

That night, we said our goodbyes. I left him half of my remaining money. The coins clattered on the table as I set them down. I quickly packed my things in a leather bag: bread, water, a second outfit, and with Jean's persistence, a study book for Latin and Arabic. I stored my birthday sword at the door and laid out my armor for the morning.

I prayed deeply, more intently than I ever had. I envisioned a battlefield bathed in the light of heaven, which would bring me clarity and salvation. I pictured a daring rescue mission, where I saved my father from some impossible Turkish fortress. Lastly, I asked God to allow me an experience that would change my life for the better.

I didn't sleep well. I probably was too excited, too energized by the deep prayers.

I awoke to a ruckus the next morning, and my heart thrummed wildly. I heard shouts and excited chatter, and smelled food. Jean was already up, and he prepared me a quick breakfast. I ate without thinking and got dressed. Being so tired but so excited was a dizzying sensation, and the pounds of armor only made it worse. I put everything on as best I could: the leather boots, tunic, mail shirt, and colorful red overcoat. With that, I gave one last goodbye to Jean. We hugged.

"Godspeed, Julien. I promise you, you'll be in my prayers every day. I hope you find what you're looking for on the other side of the water."

"Thank you, my friend." I pulled back. "And I hope you join a church or lead an abbey again. I've learned so much from you." We both smiled, and finally, I waved goodbye to a dear friend. I hoisted my bag over my shoulder, grabbed my sword, and headed outside.

Raymond and Adhemar waited there, fully equipped in their armor. I greeted my allies with an anxious yawn, but something was wrong. They were both totally still, and they glared at me. Behind them, on the main street, streams of knights marched eastward towards the docks. Their boots were like a drum, a constant heartbeat.

Why were they looking at me like that? I was already covered in sweat, and I breathed heavy in my armor. I wondered if I was stuck in some wild fever dream.

"You agree, don't you Adhemar?" Raymond asked him, but his gaze remained on me.

"I do," came the firm reply. "The boy must be forged in fire."

Raymond suddenly dashed towards me in a blur. He unsheathed his long sword. His narrowed eyes reflected a clear intent – to kill. I swallowed hard as I juggled a barrage of thoughts. What do I do? What did I do to deserve this?

That was all the time I had to think. In a reaction I hadn't quite expected, I instinctively dropped my bag and drew my sword to block the strike. The large knight shoved me backwards and I fell over. My balance was thrown off because of the extra weight.

Raymond ran at me again while Adhemar folded his arms. I scrambled to my feet as the knight struck at me again, this time faster. Though I was protected from the blade itself, I yelled out in pain with the crack that accompanied the weight of the blow. I fell to a knee.

"God, why is this happening?" I cried. Both of my allies were quiet.

Raymond drove a foot into my chest and I crashed backwards. I felt the air leave my lungs. I couldn't breathe for several agonizing seconds. When I recovered, I stared up at the clouds. I rolled over to my knees and punched the ground. I dug my knuckles into the dirt. My confusion began to fade in favor of rage.

I got to my feet, wobbly and dizzy, and heaved my sword up in front of me with one hand. Raymond's eyes were like icy daggers, and it only made my heart pound faster.

I raged forward, but he easily deflected my first attack, then my second. He crushed something into my back. It could've been another kick or his sword's hilt. Whatever it was, it was painful. I tried to use my forward momentum to roll to my feet, but I was too tired, too hot in both mind and body, to be that fluid. I ended up on my knees again.

70

"Stand, Julien," Raymond muttered. "If you wish to survive."

I stabbed my long sword into the ground to help myself up. I stared at Adhemar and Raymond. No one could help me. The knights that marched down the street sounded like a thunderstorm by this point.

As my hope of survival faded, Jean lunged out of the house. He screamed at the knights, and demanded to know why they had assaulted me. Raymond pointed his sword at the abbot, and my friend withered. But still, he rushed to my defense. He stood in front of me.

Adhemar's arms dropped to his side, and his intensity softened just a bit. Raymond, though, maintained his presence. He raised his blade, which glimmered in the morning sun, and stepped towards us. This is it, I thought. I'm dead. We're both dead. My head dropped. Thank you, Jean…

Just then, I heard a heavy footstep.

"That's enough!" Adhemar called.

I gasped and lifted my head. Raymond sheathed his sword, and his cold look disappeared. He held out his hand for me. He had to reach around Jean to do it. The abbot moved aside with a confused look on his face.

I hesitantly grabbed the knight's hand, and he pulled me to my feet. He tossed me some water. I juggled the container and managed to hang on to it. I gulped down the water.

Adhemar showed a hint of a smile as he paced up to me. "Your last test," he said.

I took a big breath and exhaled with relief. "You're kidding, right?"

"Raymond told you to be ready for anything."

"How could the boy have expected his own allies to turn on

71

him?" Jean barked.

"Julien." Raymond placed both hands on my shoulders, and I recoiled as one still throbbed in pain. "I needed you to experience that survival instinct. It was the only way for you to glimpse into the future."

"You expect us to die?" I grimaced.

"No. But we must be prepared for anything. Any horror, any betrayal. Despite the pope's certitude about our journey, I want you to be ready for the coming battles. We didn't have as much time as I wanted to train you." He glanced at Adhemar, then Jean, before he shifted his eyes back to me. "You know of our mission to find Elchanes – you want to be part of it, don't you?"

"I do, sir!" I stood up straight.

"Good. I hope this will have prepared you."

I hesitated before I asked my next question. "Sir... His Holiness was certain of our success, wasn't he? Do you doubt him?"

"Not at all." He kneeled in front of me. "But the Lord works in mysterious ways. It's apparent from the way the first wave failed – we can't simply walk over our enemies."

My voice dipped to hardly a whisper. "Okay..."

"Chin up, Julien. You will get to fulfill your dream of visiting the holy land very soon." He smiled and let me go.

"My apologies, Julien," Adhemar said. "We won't ever hurt you again. I promise."

"Thanks," I said to him. Then, with a quick, relieved breath, I gave Jean one last hug before he headed back inside.

Even with the march that rumbled through the city, there was a minute of eerie quiet as I stood with my allies. I focused on Raymond. "Sir... am I supposed to be prepared for false promises, too?"

Raymond didn't answer.

Before we joined the parade of seemingly endless knights, my allies had more gifts for me. First, Raymond tossed me a silver hemet. I hurriedly hoisted it on my head, and it only made me sweat harder. He had also brought a second shield with him. He pushed it into my chest, and I grabbed it. I as in awe. The shield bore a red color, similar to my coat, and it was marked with the words 'Soldier of Toulouse.' It seemed I had become a member of Raymond's forces.

Finally, the biggest surprise of all arrived. A Byzantine guard appeared around the corner with three horses in tow. The first two I'd seen – Raymond's gray horse, and Adhemar's darker one. The third was new to me, a smaller steed with a beautiful white coat.

"She's yours, Julien," Raymond said. "Alexios was kind enough to offer this one. You can thank him when we win this war."

"She's beautiful," Adhemar added. "An Arabian horse, I see."

"Exactly. She'll be faster than our breeds. I was hoping to get a quick one for you, in case…" He frowned. "Ah, it's nothing."

I was left stunned. I couldn't believe Raymond's generosity.

I petted my new companion to help her get used to me. I mounted and patted her side. "I hope I remember how to ride," I said.

"You'll be fine," Raymond replied. "Do you have a name in mind?"

"Hmm, I'll have to think about that." I smiled and patted the bright horse again. "It's nice to meet you, anyway, girl!"

I was overcome with happiness. The gifts had knocked my tiredness right off, and the sound of the knights' march was a drum to match my heartbeat. My new leader had one last thing to say, and he shouted it like a boom of thunder:

"Let's go – it's time to fulfill our duty! For God!"

I cheered along with the hundreds of knights who heard him.

Even though the Greeks had been suspicious of the knights, thousands of them saw us off, waving and whistling. There were certainly others who were happy to see us leave, to be rid of what they might've considered an invasion. A rare few heaved pebbles at us as they shouted and jeered. I struggled to ignore them until we made it to the port.

It took hours to get us aboard a ferry. I ended up in a long line of other soldiers. The line grew shorter and shorter as the boats took thousands of us across the Bosporus. Eventually, it was my turn.

I eased my new horse aboard and settled onto the ferry's wood. It swayed and creaked as more heavily armored men joined us. I kept close to Raymond, but there was barely any space to move. It was already hot and stuffy, and we hadn't even gotten across the water yet.

Once the ferry moved, things cooled down. I felt the breeze from the water. During the short trip, I was trapped in my mind. Raymond summoned me back to reality as he firmly tapped my shoulder.

And then, suddenly, we were there. We touched the land and the captain ushered us off the ferry. I was left on the beach, in enemy territory, with an allied army that amassed into more impossible numbers with each and every minute. I felt a surge of inspiration as knights and soldiers nearby rallied and cheered.

I gazed out in the distance, to this unknown land. It was rugged and mountainous, with nature as far as the eye could see.

The massive Catholic war machine marched along the worn trail before us. The different faces, equipment, and energies all merged together into one blurry memory. Raymond and I watched in amazement. I imagined what the Turks would do when they witnessed this.

Alexios came up behind us and patted me on the shoulder as he passed by on his horse. "It's quite a sight, isn't it?" he said with a grin.

"It's something out of a dream…" I quietly replied.

"I wish your army well. As promised, I'll make camp behind your forces and offer support where I can."

"Thank you, Your Grace," Raymond said.

Alexios bowed his head and returned towards the water. He kept a watchful eye on our army.

Godfrey approached us, flanked by Bohemond and Tancred. "Are you lot going to simply wait there?" he asked us. "Or are you going to get moving? The Turks' capital isn't far off."

"We'll get there," Raymond replied as he turned his horse away. "Don't worry about us. Go on ahead to Nicaea. We have a mission to take care of."

"I don't need your approval." Godfrey smirked. "I'll see you there – if you can make it."

Raymond simply held a hand up towards the obnoxious Frenchman.

Adhemar approached next. "Sir Raymond, we shall see you up ahead. May God be with you."

My mentor raised his head with a smile. "Yes, you too. See you soon."

The other leaders took off ahead of us. The bulk of the army continued with them, and there were plenty more on the way. Raymond summoned several men to his side, a collection of his own soldiers. They gathered, close to a hundred strong.

"Men, listen up!" Raymond called. "You're coming with the three of us. We're taking a detour."

"A detour, sir?" came a question from one soldier.

"Yes. Consider it a special assignment from the Lord himself."

The men were charged up by that detail, which hadn't surprised me. I would've been too if I hadn't known already.

"We're to locate the camp of an enemy general – Elchanes. The last we've heard, he's stationed at a castle garrison to the west." Raymond shifted on his horse and tensed one gauntleted hand into a fist. "He's responsible for the murder of Catholics – our French brothers who arrived here before us. So, my friends, we're going to kill him and anyone with him. We're going to burn his camp to the ground. Are you with me?" He raised his fist.

"Aye!" the men collectively cheered.

I was fired up, too. I raised my shoulders, and Raymond looked at me. "I'm with you, sir!"

Our first mission in hostile territory was set.

We'd only drifted away from the countless soldiers nearby when I noticed something along the top of a sun-soaked mountain ridge in front of us.

A group of Turks. There were about a dozen of them, with black horses and equally dark armor. They peered down on our army.

"Sir Raymond! Look, on the ridge!"

He'd already seen them. Thousands of heads turned to see what we did.

One man among the enemy might've been a leader. He was at the front of a V-shaped formation. I could've sworn he stared at me, but he was too far away to tell.

"Men, get up there!" Raymond called as he pointed at the ridge. "Only a small section. I don't want everyone charging into a trap! You see what's up there, and then you report back – clear?"

Cheers and roars broke out in our forces. But the men were disciplined. Only a small group raced off after our enemies.

76

I was thrust into an emotional frenzy. I squeezed my reins and prepared to jolt ahead, but Raymond grabbed my arm. "Not you, Julien. You want to abandon the mission already?"

I eased up beside him, feeling like I had been hit with cold water. "Sorry. I thought we were under attack."

"Not yet." Raymond peered back at the ridge, and my eyes followed his. The Turks were gone. In the distance, the soldiers climbed the side of the mountain, struggling in heavy armor. "It could be an ambush. But perhaps they were just observing us. Either way, they would've known we were coming."

I took a heavy breath. "Right."

Once the knights made it atop the ridge, they signaled that things were clear. As we continued west, I looked back over my shoulder at the endless line of soldiers, women, priests and horses as they got farther away. I headed deeper into the unknown with only about a hundred people. It definitely felt strange. I desperately wanted to find my father. I wondered whether this path would lead to him, if he could somehow be alive – a survivor.

Chapter 8

By nightfall, Anatolia was an entirely different place.

I had already experienced the warm, pristine sunlight of the day, but at night it was almost pitch-black. There was no moon to light the way, and unfamiliar animals made noises foreign to my ears. Odd insects buzzed by me, and I swatted them away anxiously.

My knightly companions were undisturbed, though, as the near one hundred of them marched with Raymond and me. Aside from the waves that washed over the coast, their heavy boots were the only thing I could follow, an ever-present drum I felt within my heart.

We walked for hours with few breaks, and my body ached from the strain of my armor. We prepared to rest when one of the knights saw a light in the distance. To my tired eyes, it looked like a mirage, an orange beacon sent by the heavens.

The knights drew their weapons, which startled me, and snapped me to attention.

We approached a grassy ridge, and then Raymond quietly ordered our group to stay low. We hopped down from our horses. I petted my new steed as calmly as I could, but she recoiled from my touch. She must have sensed my nerves.

As I crouched in the heavy armor, it was nearly twice the strain, but I pushed on and followed my mentor as best I could.

When we came over the ridge, we had a view of the light's source: a Seljuk camp. There were no enemies, but the remnants of the occupants were plain to see – and what I saw surprised me.

Aside from the still-lit campfires, there was food out, ready to be eaten. Fallen cups lay strewn about, and a few horses remained, neighing faintly in the distance. There were dozens of tents, which could have been from any camp I'd seen thus far. The only thing that definitively marked it as an enemy camp was a collection of weapons, which Raymond noted: unusual curved blades were spiked into the grass.

Raymond suddenly said, "If any of you spot one of those bastard Turks, don't hesitate to take their heads. I don't care who they are, men, women, or children." I looked at him with a cold sweat on my forehead. The knights nearest to me tensed their fists, and nodded firmly. My mentor's eyes were frightening as he added, "The only survivors will be the ones with information. Once we're done, we'll dispose of them, too."

The knights passed the hushed orders between our group, and Raymond kept his eyes on me. His words had pierced my soul. He had told me back in Constantinople what he'd expected of me – of us, on this journey – but I don't think it had really sunk in until now. I cast my gaze out over the camp again, at a place where clearly our enemies had been recently.

I realized then that these were people we were fighting. People who had likely fled at the sight of our arrival – our massive march down the roads of Anatolia. If they were unholy, why would they run? Could it really be as simple – as cruel – as my allies had said?

I had been right to question things, but I had also terribly underestimated the courage of the Turks.

Soon after my troubled thoughts began to linger, I heard a distant rumble, like thunder. It was no storm. The sound came from two directions.

"Ambush!" Raymond cried. The knights collectively sprung to their feet, with me last to react. "Back to the horses, men!"

We slid back down the other side of the ridge and raced to our horses. Just as we arrived, we realized we were surrounded.

The Turks encircled us like shadowy streaks across a canvas. One of them called out in their blur of horses:

"Turn back."

"We won't allow you to destroy our people, or our home," another cried.

"This is your one chance to retreat," a third boomed.

They spoke in Arabic, of course, and none of my allies seemed to understand. Then, the Turks appeared to open a section of their forces – a path out, where we might retreat. But rather than respond in words or patience, we readied our weapons for war.

That was when the rain of arrows started.

I'd never experienced anything like it. My first reaction was a yelp of terror, the desperate cry of the child I was, as I felt something bounce off of my back. Thankfully, it hadn't struck me dead-on.

A few of the knights screamed. It was the first of many death cries I would hear. The first, though, might have been the worst. Several armored bodies collapsed behind us, and a few of our horses scattered as the rest of the knights took to theirs. Raymond grabbed my arm and helped me aboard my own as the second volley came from the Turks.

This time, one knight fell. He plummeted lifelessly off of his horse in a heap. I struggled to keep my emotion inside as I held up

81

my shield, and desperately gripped my horse's reigns with the other.

I felt like I was trapped in a dream, but as another arrow crashed upon my shield, I knew this was reality. The one we had created.

As the Turks prepared another round of fire, Raymond called, "Find your courage, my friends! We can win this battle. We outnumber the infidel!"

How does he know that? I frantically wondered. I could hardly focus on one thing, let alone the whole battle, but the fact that Raymond had so calmly determined the enemy's numbers sent an unexpected surge of hope through me.

The knights roared in response to our leader, and we began to chase the Turks. They wheeled and retreated, still able to aim and fire their bows as they pulled away from us, and they took down one more knight in the barrage that followed.

Soon, the tides turned. My allies were bloodthirsty. They caught up to the Turks and hacked away at them. Eventually, their violent blows landed, and scores of Turks toppled to the earth, dead.

I was lost, afraid, and my mind spun. I barely managed to track Raymond, and I stuck to him like I was one of his limbs. As hopelessness settled in my heart, my mentor pulled up short, and his horse bucked. I trotted beside him, and he stared at me intensely.

With the sounds of death and mayhem around us, Raymond coldly said, "You must rise up against this challenge, Julien – for God."

"Sir?" I stuttered.

His eyes burrowed into my very soul. "Stand aside, or else you'll be killed." Then he raced back into the fray, and I was left stunned and frozen.

I simply found cover. I realized I would be completely useless in the battle.

To my surprise, the skirmish ended quickly. The Turks were

elegant and deadly, but our armor was our advantage. Their arrows often ricocheted off of our iron and stuck out harmlessly from our thick coats. Eventually, the dozens of Turks were cut down, one by one, and I felt nauseous and weak.

A stray few Turks got away. They fled into the pitch-black night, and the knights were enraged and unsatisfied. Raymond decided to direct their anger elsewhere.

The knights set the camp on fire. We threw torches into tents and burned any nearby nature that would serve to strengthen the flames. I looked on, lost in the orange inferno, and wondered what my duty was, what my purpose was. But then, something happened that would set me free.

Several people emerged from the most distant tents, about ten unarmed Turks. And one other person: a young girl. She wore a long, dark-blue dress and a head covering.

The knights moved in and killed two of the survivors in a cruel flurry of violence. They demanded the surrender of the others. I followed much more quickly than I had in the battle before.

Raymond descended from his horse, and many of the knights did the same, including me. He stepped up to the group of survivors and pressed his sword right to the lead man's neck.

"Where is Elchanes?" he shouted.

"Please, spare us," the Seljuk warrior replied. "We can't understand you! You're asking about Elchanes? We don't know where he is!"

Raymond's face twisted in disgust, though I had a strong suspicion he didn't know what the man said. I approached him.

"Sir, I… I can translate."

"Oh, so now you wish to be useful?" my mentor said. Some of the knights laughed, and with the roar of the fire over their voices, they sounded like they were from a nightmare.

"I do, sir."

"Go on."

I complied. I relayed the Arabic messages as best I could.

The knight ran his blade along the man's neck and said, "You say you don't know where your general is? I think you're telling the truth. Well, if you don't know, then none of you are of use to me. It's about time we finish this..." Raymond pressed the blade in more firmly.

Fear overwhelmed me, but my eyes drifted to the girl, who stared back at me with tears in her eyes. She was a pale ghost, as if her spirit had flown away.

This massacre might have been called God's work, but it didn't feel that way to me. The girl's tears touched my very soul, and sent a spark of courage to my heart.

"I can't agree to this!" I called. I dropped my sword and shield, and removed my helmet.

"Steel yourself, Julien!" Raymond barked. "This is what we came here to do. This is our duty!"

"Is this what the Lord would want? To wipe out those who surrender? To kill defenseless girls?" My eyes hadn't moved from her. My emotions spiraled out of control.

"So you want to take responsibility, Julien?" My mentor grabbed my shoulders. "Look at me."

I obeyed.

"After you abandoned your responsibility in the battle before – you want it now? You want to take the lives of these fools into your hands?"

"Sir," I shouted. "I do, sir."

"Why?" The question was emotionless, sharp like a dagger. I

still wonder if my mentor actually cared to hear my response.

I looked over the survivors, each of them, and they looked back in gaping terror. These people weren't unholy – they were human beings. When I returned my eyes to Raymond, he had moved away.

"Fine, Julien. I will grant your request." He glared at the Turks as if they were less than human. Then, he peered at me in almost the same way. "If any of them come back to cause us harm… I will deal with you myself. Do you understand me?"

I surprised myself by how quickly I answered, "I understand."

My surprise doubled as, almost without realizing it, I approached the girl.

"Miss," I said as I knelt beside her. The girl recoiled. I held my hands up and asked, "Is there any chance you understand me?"

She hesitated. "Yes…"

I slowly nodded. "I… I know nothing I could say would be enough for you, to ease the pain of what we've done here. But I am sorry."

My words summoned more laughter from my allies. They hadn't understood a word I'd said, but the fact that I was even trying to communicate must've amused them. This time, I found myself angry instead of unnerved.

"Please, go," I continued. "Try to find someplace safe."

The girl slapped me. The blow was quick and harsh, but I accepted it, and slowly turned my face back to her. She said, "There will never be safety in a war for God."

I nodded, and a tear streamed down my face. It disappeared quickly in the growing heat. Truly, even in the chaos of my thoughts, I knew she was right.

"Ugh, can't we just finish them off?" another knight yelled.

"No!" Raymond replied. "The decision is made." He flicked

his head at the fearful victims. "So go. Get out, all of you!" The Turks were frozen in fear. The knight sighed deeply. "I disagree with this, Julien."

"I know what you said to me before, but... is there no room for mercy, sir?"

"It's not merciful to free them. They will live in terror until they're killed by our army. Don't you see, boy? This war will burn everything away."

Amidst more laughter and disagreement from the knights, the survivors fled from the circle, and headed towards the darkness beyond the fires.

We left the camp behind, and the knights cheered and sung songs in glee. As for me, I stopped atop the ridge. I observed our bloody battlefield, and then turned back to witness our fiery destruction one last time. Tents fell into cinders as choking smoke filled the air and wafted towards the sky.

My heart ached, but then it dropped. The girl had collapsed, and the others continued to flee.

I pressed a heavy boot into the dirt, almost ready to help her myself, but then someone else emerged from the shadows: another Turk.

He threw off his helmet and dropped to his knees near the girl. He frantically screamed, "Zahra! Zahra!" He shook her. "Sister!"

He lifted her into his arms, with a face covered in dancing shadows from the flames. A moment later, we met eyes.

The tears ran freely down his cheeks, but his eyes were so dark, so terrible, filled with imaginable hatred – towards us, and towards me. He looked so young, like me. But behind that, I knew he was capable of fighting – capable of defending his home. His presence carried that truth. It rivaled the scorching flames that surrounded him.

His vengeful intent lingered on me, our gazes trapped within one another's, and then finally, he retreated with his sister in his arms.

I turned back to join my allies, who by now had all but left me behind.

Chapter 9

We left the massacre behind.

We hadn't found the general, Elchanes, and there was no trail to follow, so we set out to meet our main army at Nicaea. On the way, we stayed in a tight-knit formation in case we were attacked from the darkness. Most of the knights were still happy, charged from the killing and the fires. As for me, it was impossible to avoid the tension between Raymond and myself. We hadn't said a word between us for hours.

My first battle had been something of a rite of passage into the army, and I had failed, according to the knights. When the first Turks fell and we set the camp on fire, I hadn't felt excited – I had felt sick.

Worse, I hadn't secured a kill, and I threw away any chance to earn goodwill when I offered to spare the survivors. I caught the cold glances, the murmurs behind my back. Who was I to these warriors beside me? I was a child who took advantage of his leader.

I didn't know what to think. Nothing had gone the way I expected. The Turks were no devils. They had families. Siblings.

The truth was, every time I blinked, I saw the terrified face of the Muslim girl. I felt her hand on my cheek from her slap. Her deep brown eyes remained locked with mine, though we were long separated.

Despite the opposition, even from Raymond, my heart told me there had to be something more to this war. If we killed everyone in our way, how could we possibly be better than the enemy we were supposed to hate? I was alone in asking that question, it seemed.

Loneliness pressed in, squeezing me like the dark night of Anatolia.

We passed through a stretch of trees with a small lake in the middle. I hopped off my horse and led her away from the group to wash my face. I looked at my reflection, but I only saw the girl in the water.

Despite her fear, despite her anger, I had actually thought she was beautiful. For a fleeting moment, I wondered what her smile would look like. I washed my face with the cool water.

I got up to pet my horse, and I remembered that I hadn't decided on a name for her. I couldn't think. My mind frantically raced. "Am I going crazy?" I said to her. "Why am I still thinking about that girl?"

She reared her head back and dug a hoof into the dirt a few times.

"Yeah, I guess I am losing it." I quietly laughed.

I rejoined my allies and trailed a little behind the group. I was surprised to find that Raymond had searched for me.

"There you are! Where'd you get off to?"

"Oh," I stammered. "I just went to wash up. I thought..."

He half-smiled. "You thought what, that we were enemies after our disagreement?"

"No, I..." I held a hand up.

"The past few hours have simply been a time for reflection. Don't worry, Julien."

I felt a swell of positivity. "That is heartening. It's just… I see the way some of the knights look at me."

"They don't know you like I do. You have a good heart, but… if you're going to be kind, you'd better expect this. I told you before – we've come here to kill. That is what God has asked of us, of you."

I slowly nodded. I tried to allow that grim possibility to sink into my being, and then we rejoined our group.

We traveled for perhaps another hour before we found the main trail towards Nicaea. The ground was well-trod with innumerable footsteps, probably the boots of our army.

We rounded a ridge and suddenly I smelled something foul. I groaned.

The horrible sight came into view: countless bodies piled up in stacks. They were buried in a graveyard of arrows. The collective shock hit the knights, and I heard a hundred different questions all asking what had happened here.

I wondered if our army ahead of us had taken losses. Raymond dispelled that notion.

"These must be the remains of the first wave," he said. "The peasants who marched out ahead of us."

Dread overwhelmed me. Was my father in there somewhere?

Raymond grabbed hold of me. "Listen to me, Julien. The only way you're going to find an answer is to go digging through those bodies. You don't want to do that, do you?" He knelt and looked right into my eyes.

"N-no, sir. I couldn't…" My eyes welled with tears.

"So instead – we pray for these departed souls. We make them proud. We carry on their will to victory."

"Yes, sir…"

"Stay strong, son. If your father is out there – he'd want you to be."

I cried, but with Raymond's help, I found the strength to press on.

Our journey continued under a crescent moon that emerged from behind the clouds. Out in the distance, there was a massive city. It reminded me of the fortress, Constantinople – only slightly less imposing. Nearby, there was a huge camp that contained the bulk of our army. The glint of moonlight off bright armor was unmistakable.

My heart sunk at seeing what was between the two landmarks: another field of blood and broken corpses. This time, like before, there were both knights and Turks.

We signaled to our allies as we got close. They had chopped down some nearby trees, and built siege engines to bring the walls down.

The aggressive Godfrey hailed us first. He may as well have had steam coming out of his ears.

"Where in God's name have you been?"

"My apologies, Godfrey," Raymond said with a bow of his head. "We had our mission to complete."

"That sounds like a load of horseshit to me."

Angered shouts echoed out from our knights, but things settled quickly when Raymond raised a hand. "Sir Godfrey, you know me well enough – I would never abandon this fight."

"You're lucky Pope Urban seems to fancy you. Very lucky."

"Get on your way, or we're going to have a problem."

Godfrey stormed into one of the tents, while the tall and stoic Adhemar approached us next.

"I was worried about you," he said. "So you were on a mission, is that right? The one you mentioned to Alexios?"

"Yes," Raymond replied. "We were hunting the general – Elchanes."

"Ahh. You tracked him down?"

"No. We found a camp and fought off an ambush, but there was no sign of him."

"You've lost men, haven't you? I can see it in your eyes."

My mentor sniffed hard and looked away. "I'll take it out on the Turks."

"We shall pray for the fallen, in the meantime." Adhemar bowed his head. "Is your mission on hold, then?"

"That's right," Raymond continued. "We were going to continue the search, but I wondered if Elchanes retreated here. That, and I had a feeling the war would get underway."

"Your instincts were right." Adhemar paused and shifted to observe the field of bodies. "The Turks' leader appeared to fight us – he called himself Kilij Arslan. He took the time to announce himself as he battered us with arrows. We made him retreat, but... not without some difficult losses." He sighed deeply.

My eyes were locked on the battlefield. "It's a good sign that you pushed away their leader, though, isn't it?"

"Yes. But I plan to get the siege underway tonight. If we can secure this city, Jerusalem will be easy by comparison." He turned to me and tilted his head. "Julien, you look unwell. What's the matter?"

Raymond spoke first, although I wouldn't have been quick to answer. "The boy found some kindness out at the camp. He offered to spare a few survivors."

"Is that so?" Adhemar brought a hand to his chin. "You agreed to this, Raymond?"

"On the condition that he accepts responsibility."

"Why did you do that, Julien?" Adhemar kept an intent gaze

on me.

"We won the skirmish," I said. "The survivors surrendered, and... there was a girl among them."

"I see." He observed our group of knights. Some grumbled in discontent. He raised his voice and continued, "Perhaps it's a good idea to learn something from young Julien here."

The knights stood at attention, and whispers of uncertainty broke out.

"It is simply this," Adhemar continued. "There is duty, and then there is malice. We are here to fight for God, but we must also carry His light and love."

"But is the enemy not evil?" came a resounding call from a knight.

"Perhaps. There will come a time when we bring hell to them... that will be at Jerusalem. It will be due on that day."

"And until then?" another shouted.

"We crush the enemy. But if they surrender, we show them that we are the greater warriors – by allowing them to do that."

The murmurs in the crowd continued, but I was amazed that Adhemar supported me. Finally, he left us with a booming rallying cry. "My friends, we are the strongest army on this earth. Nicaea is already trembling – you can feel it, can't you? We'll bring it to the ground with God on our side! For we burn with passion for our faith, for our Lord – we burn with God!"

Mighty cheers resounded through our group. It pushed away my concern and made the moon seem brighter, even if it was all in the mind.

We returned to the tents. The army was set for its first real fight. The pent-up aggression was almost palpable. Swords were drawn, and the sharp metal sound echoed around me. Battle plans were verbally passed from group to group, person to person: we were to charge to the walls with the siege equipment and break through the gates. The cavalry would stay behind to avoid arrow fire.

Raymond met with me, and he grabbed my arms on either side. "Are you ready this time?"

I exhaled deeply. In my mind, I was uncertain – but the energy in camp was an unavoidable surge. And truly, I still wanted desperately for things to be easy. I eventually said, "I am."

My mentor grabbed me tighter. He could've crushed me if he wanted to. "Say it again, Julien."

This time, I repeated it more firmly: "I am."

He pushed an iron fist into my chest with a big smile. "Good. We'll need you. Stick by me, all right?" I nodded.

I heard a low rumble. The men stomped their feet and tapped their shields. It became a rhythm, and I felt it in my body. The leaders of the army took to the center of camp: Raymond, Adhemar, Godfrey, along with the gruff Bohemond and Tancred from Italy.

"My dear friends," Raymond shouted, "we've waited for this day for a long time. This is the day the truth will become evident – we are righteous, doing our duty for a just God!"

The thumping rose in pace and pitch, and a powerful cheer accompanied it. It vibrated through me like a lightning bolt.

"The Muslims have already thrown their best at us," Godfrey added. "Their foolish sultan was bested by his betters! They have no hope left!"

"Stand tall," Bohemond said as he drew the frighteningly large sword from his back. "We will obliterate the non-believers and send them to hell!"

Another cheer resounded in the night. I found myself affected, and I almost joined in.

"Together," Adhemar cried, "we can achieve anything! Men — let us march! For God!"

"For God!" the cries of innumerable men pierced the air, and this time it included mine. I couldn't deny that my journey hadn't appeared divine, but in my ignorant imagination, this was the picture of holy.

In reality, it was a broken vision of righteousness.

Nicaea had been a threatening sight, but at that moment, I didn't feel a shred of fear. I readied my sword and shield.

Our army continued in a stream for a few hundred feet and then spread out to encircle Nicaea. I remained close to my familiar group. We were on the frontlines, looking towards the tall gates of Nicaea.

Not a moment later, the Turks poured out on their horses. I couldn't count how many, but it was only a drop in our ocean. The gates closed behind them, and the towers remained full of enemies.

"Men!" Adhemar screamed. "To battle!"

We roared, a collective fearsome cry, and then we charged. I was swept up in the aggression of war.

The Turks outside the walls raced out to meet us. They let arrows loose, with hundreds that sailed into the sky above and dropped down on us like rain. My group held up their shields and braced for impact. My shield vibrated and crashed into my arm as the arrows pelted me.

I darted my eyes back to the battle. Hundreds of horse archers were headed our way. They let another volley fly, with a frightful whoosh that pierced the air. I kept my shield up, but an arrow dropped right into my shoulder. I shrieked and fell to a knee. My shield bounced in the dirt.

I couldn't move my arm.

Adhemar sprinted to me and grabbed my shield. He held it up

to protect us from another deadly wave of arrows. I heard screams from some of our allies.

"Take out those horse archers!" Adhemar shouted.

Our side returned fire, and a section of the enemy and their horses went down. The Turks quickly maneuvered away.

I blinked quickly a few times, as if I was seeing an illusion: one of the enemies had a girl with him on his horse. It was Zahra. And then, I realized that it was her brother on the horse.

A jolt of pain went through my body, and I gritted my teeth. Did this mean the survivors came back to fight us? If so, Raymond would have my head.

I searched for my mentor. His voice carried as he shouted orders to our archers. When I glanced back, the girl sat on a different horse – and her brother galloped towards us with a shockingly small group.

They attacked with a quick volley of arrows, and four knights around me toppled to their deaths. I wanted to help, but I was losing strength. Worse, Zahra's brother charged right towards me.

Our forces must've been preparing to fire, as there were no arrows to save me. The enemy group collided with our front line, swords on shields. One rider made contact with Raymond. My leader lashed out at him with his long sword. He grunted as he dueled for his life. I couldn't help. The girl's sibling suddenly jumped off his horse – and right at me.

I braced myself. He crashed on top of me and grabbed hold of my arms. I didn't have the strength to push him away. I glared at him, at his black eyes, and only saw the fires of hatred. But slowly, as we remained locked together, those flames dimmed.

"You understand me?" he said, as rain washed down his face and onto mine.

I nodded, unable to get free no matter how I tried.

"You let her go. For that, I might just offer my thanks."

"What?" I groaned through terrible pain.

"I'm Ahtmar. This moment – I had to see you. I had to look into your eyes."

"Why?" I cried.

"You aren't like them. But… I can't see past what you've done." His words seemed to hurt him. He held his curved sword above me. "We are even now, Julien. But next time – I don't know what will happen."

A heartbeat later, he pushed off of me and deftly maneuvered to his feet. Our archers fired another round at the enemy, but they missed the scattered group. Raymond roared as he fought off his attacker, who spun his horse around and retreated. My mentor dashed over to me in a brilliant blur and slammed his blade into Ahtmar's.

The two violently clashed. They deflected blows from one another and locked swords. Raymond was three times the size of Ahtmar, but the boy moved quickly, like a rush of water. He avoided my mentor's attacks at every turn.

Raymond jumped back to me in time for another enemy volley. He shielded us both. Stray arrows pierced the dirt right near my head.

The knight raced ahead to resume his battle with Ahtmar, while I worked my way to my feet. Despite the pain, I wanted to give more for this fight, and I had been swept into its dark gravity. The knight jockeyed to break Ahtmar's guard, so I ran in and aimed a strike at his body. He pulled back, but Raymond and I pushed ahead once more. We both swung at him in tandem from the left and right. My mentor slashed Ahtmar's side, and the boy toppled over. Apparently, it had only grazed him since the boy quickly sprung back to his feet.

The rain picked up, and the wind howled. Somewhere in all the noise I heard Zahra cry, "Brother!" Her words froze me in my tracks.

Ahtmar gave me a long look before he whistled for his horse and slipped away with the rest of his group. They escaped with their lives, but not without wounds. Among their night-colored outfits, I spotted Zahra again as she hopped on Ahtmar's horse. She and I made eye contact, and my heart felt heavy from her ghostly expression. Finally, their group rejoined the main force of horse archers, whose numbers dropped with each passing minute.

Our armies traded arrows for what felt like hours. Each time, we got a little closer to the walls, and lost a few more men. It was odd. After enduring tens of volleys, the fire within me dimmed. I wasn't certain if my strength had given out, or if I had quickly adjusted to battle, and I didn't know which thought was worse.

I heard a heavy clank. Something rolled up behind me. As I glanced back, I saw our battering ram on its approach. It was a collection of wood shaped in a triangle, with a massive log in the center. Over a dozen soldiers pushed the huge thing from the back. There were two other engines as well, headed for different parts of the wall.

We'd staved off the horse archers. Most of them retreated back into the city gates, which quickly opened and shut behind them. Ahtmar's group didn't enter Nicaea, though – instead, they sought freedom through a weaker section of our army. I watched from the distance, with no horse of my own at the moment. Their twenty or so horses crashed through a collection of our knights twice their size. But they didn't all escape – a few were cut down by blades and maces. The rest pushed on to a ridge overlooking the city.

They watched us, quietly and solemnly. I kept my eyes on Zahra until Ahtmar's group was chased away by our forces. In the madness, I wondered if Nicaea was the girl's home.

I remember losing track of things after that. It was hard to stay focused with the death all around as I pictured Zahra, again and again.

I remained under Raymond's protection. He breathed heavier each time he blocked a volley of arrows.

Finally, we made it to the walls, and the rams were in position. I pressed up against the rain-soaked stone, and looked across at Raymond, whose eyes burned with intensity.

We both watched the closest ram in action. The engineers pulled back the log and slammed it into the gates with a boom that was louder than the worst thunder. It vibrated through the stone and through me. The enemies above us screamed, but they persisted. More arrows came our way, and they hurled rocks down at us.

I hunkered down. My leader slid along the wall to the ram, and called out, "The gate is starting to crack! Keep up the pressure!"

I braced myself for the next vibration. Even so, my ears rang and my teeth clattered. A cheer emanated from around me as wood crumbled down to the earth from the gates. Our cavalry marched in behind us. Alexios arrived with them, flanked by another huge wave of soldiers.

It was a brilliant sight, an image that's still coated in a holy light in my memory – though I know it wasn't the reality. But it accompanied the rising sun, a new dawn, and what happened next: the call that signaled the end of the battle.

"We surrender!"

It was a collection of voices that all pleaded the same thing from the towers above. We let loose a mighty victory cry, one that I happily joined.

Then, after the emotional outpour, a chilling silence fell. Alexios raced up to the gates with a select few of his guards. He turned back and looked over our inspired but tired army. In the quiet, I heard groans of pain and exhausted breaths before the gates of Nicaea were opened. On the other side, I saw defeated faces – sad, fearful, and ashamed. Their weapons were dropped to the ground. The emperor of Constantinople stood between our army and a conquering raid.

"Well done," he said, slowly nodding. "Truly, you are fine warriors."

"What is the meaning of this?" Raymond called as he strode up to the emperor's horse. "We're going to enter the city – and claim what's ours."

"No. You're not."

Byzantine soldiers marched through the middle of our army. They parted us like water. They were a black stream among the silver knights.

Godfrey grabbed Alexios by the arm, but he was quickly shoved away by the emperor's guards.

"You would deprive us of our spoils?" the Frenchman shrieked.

"You'll have your supplies," Alexios calmly replied. "But you'll not march into this city and massacre my people."

"Your people...?"

Bohemond raised a fist. "What if we crush you too, then, Alexios?" A significant cheer erupted from the knights with the giant.

"The people inside Nicaea are not all Muslim," he said, ignoring Bohemond. "Many are my citizens – Christians. This used to be my city. So would you walk inside and slaughter everyone – even Christians?"

Tancred shadowed Bohemond, and the young man shook his head. "They're not truly faithful."

"Ahh," Alexios muttered. He raised his voice into a roar, "Now we see how narrow-minded you are! No, we'll not fight over this

– I wouldn't be as foolish as you to do that. Remember this, you crusaders: you owe your loyalty to me!"

I was at a loss. I tried to bring my hands together in prayer, but my wounded arm wouldn't move.

Adhemar approached Alexios and stood beside him.

"My friends!" he called. "Let us make peace today. Remember what we spoke about – there is duty, and there is malice!"

His words were akin to being dropped into a frigid bath. It took some contemplation, a long delay from the hungry, angry knights, but the leaders conceded – if anything because they had made vows to Alexios.

It was an uncertain moment for me – one I was happy to share in common with the emperor. I didn't want to massacre a city, especially a Christian city. But then, I'd found I couldn't stand any death, even those of my supposed enemies.

Alexios continued, "I am appointing a general to oversee Nicaea. If you plan to enter for any reason, you'll do so ten men at a time. Otherwise, we'll be bringing your supplies up from the coast soon – then you can continue on your way."

I gazed up towards the ridge Ahtmar's group had retreated to earlier. They had returned. Their weapons were drawn, but they remained still. Zahra's arms were wrapped around her brother. I wondered if they heard what Alexios said. I remembered that Zahra actually had understood my words back at the camp. I hoped for another chance to speak to her.

It was around then that I began to feel ill – the pain had become too much. Moments later, I collapsed into darkness.

Chapter 10

I awoke to the smell of honey and the dim light of a candle beside me. My body ached and throbbed unlike anything I'd ever felt before. My instinct was to sit up, but I didn't have the strength. Instead, I groaned and fell back the one inch I'd moved in the unfamiliar bed.

"Easy now, Julien," Adhemar said. His calm voice settled me. At least I knew I was in safe hands.

"Sir Adhemar," I weakly replied. "Where are you? I can't tilt my head down."

"Here." He sat forward in his chair and looked down at me with a soft smile. "We almost lost you."

My memories flooded back to me. I placed my hand on my wounded shoulder, but there was no arrow. I felt bandages instead. "You got the arrow out?"

"No, not me. This young lady here." He raised his head as a girl approached the other side of my bed.

She was small, with long, messy black hair that peeked through a hijab like Zahra's. Her warm, brown eyes reflected the gentle candlelight.

"Hello," she said with a smile. "Julien, wasn't it?"

"Uh, yes!" I was suddenly embarrassed with the lady at my bedside.

"He's a funny one, isn't he?" She glanced at Adhemar, who frowned.

"I don't understand your language," he muttered.

I refocused on the young lady. "What's your name, miss?"

"Sabuhi. Good to meet you."

"You helped me?"

"I did."

"Thank you. Where are we, anyway?"

"Nicaea." She glanced away.

I blinked quickly a few times. "This is your home, isn't it?" I pushed through my pain and sat up on my elbows. "Why did you help me?"

She brushed some dust off of her long, brown dress. "It's my job. I care for the wounded, no matter who they are."

I scanned the room and saw ten or so other blood-soaked beds, which were occupied by victims of the battle – both Muslims and Catholics.

"You're treating your enemies? But we… I mean, we planned to raid the city…"

"I know." Sabuhi looked at me sternly, and her eyes glimmered with wisdom beyond her age. She seemed to be just a teenager, but she must've seen a lot in her life. "But we've coexisted with your people – your faith – for some time. It's not that strange to be assisting Christians, or Catholics."

"Uh… okay." Her comment sailed over my head at the time.

Adhemar interrupted. "What is she saying to you, Julien? I'd prefer not to be kept out of this discussion."

"Sorry," I said as I turned my head to him. "She said it's her job

104

to help the wounded."

"I see. All right. Tell her she has my thanks for saving you. And ask how long your recovery will take – you'd like to know that, right?"

"Yes, I understand." I followed the knight's instructions, and Sabuhi expressed some concern about my recovery. It wouldn't be quick, at the very least.

Adhemar placed a hand on my arm. "You should rest, Julien."

"Okay. What's going on in the city, though?"

"Don't worry about that. Things are settling down. I'll come back to check on you tomorrow – we won't leave you behind."

Adhemar left for the day. I tried to get comfortable as I adjusted to my new surroundings. There were no windows, so I couldn't tell night from day. I only had Sabuhi's company, and she was so much kinder than I deserved. She brought me food and water, and undid my bandages every few hours to clean my wound. As I faded in and out of dreams, I thought I heard her cry.

I was awakened by the sounds of a door creaking open and closed. Sabuhi's small footsteps pattered along the wood floor, and then she greeted someone in another room.

"Hello. You're here for Julien, right?"

A coarse grunt came in reply – it was Raymond. He didn't understand the young lady, but he heard my name. "Show me to Julien."

With each word, the voices sounded closer, until I saw my mentor at my bedside. He held out a cold iron hand for me.

"Glad you made it. I was worried about you."

"Thank you, sir." I grabbed his hand, and he slowly pulled me until I sat up. I grimaced throughout. "Well, that's a start."

Sabuhi took a cloth to her hands, which were stained a deep red, and looked at me with a half-smile. An older woman entered the room with a quick pace, and she tended to the other wounded. Knowing Sabuhi wasn't the only caregiver gave me relief. At least that duty wasn't left to one person.

Raymond noticed I was distracted. "Come on, Julien. You'd better wake up. This war has only just begun."

"Yes…" I quietly replied. "You're right."

"Try to get to your feet. I want to take you outside today."

"Okay, sir." I slowly angled my legs to the right and set my bare feet onto the floor. I tensed my legs and tried to stand. I was able to, though I was wobbly.

"Get yourself dressed. In full armor. I'll see you outside." Raymond turned to Sabuhi. "Hey, girl – where are you keeping the boy's clothes?" Sabuhi didn't respond. Raymond's tone was mean and coarse. He tapped his silver chainmail. "Armor?" he continued. "Do you hear me?"

She motioned to a wooden chest near her feet. Raymond patted me on the arm before he left. The door opened and slammed shut, and there was an awkward silence as I gathered my heavy equipment.

"Sorry, Sabuhi," I said. "I think he should have been a little nicer."

"It's okay," she replied. "Thank you."

"And thank you, for everything you've done for me. I'm not sure how this happened… but I will remember you."

"I'll remember you too. You're one of the only warriors I've met with a working brain."

"Hmm?"

"It doesn't hurt to think for yourself, sometimes."

I had been too unsteady, and too foolish, to appreciate what this girl had said. I simply nodded without understanding. After a pause, Sabuhi continued.

"There was a boy like you, who lived here… I hope he's all

right. I miss him. He was always nice to me."

"Who?"

"Ahtmar. Another hopeless child."

I raised my head. I truly didn't know what to say. I only knew the person who we had hurt, and who probably wanted to hurt us back. I finished getting dressed, and the mail shirt felt especially heavy on me.

"You shouldn't be going out in your armor," Sabuhi added. She pressed a hand to her shoulder. "It'll put a lot of pressure there."

"You're right," I said. "But I don't really have a choice. I have to keep moving."

"All right then. Don't say I didn't warn you." She smiled.

I smiled back. "Thank you again, Sabuhi. I hope to see you again."

"You shouldn't count on it. But I feel the same."

I bowed my head and took my leave. When I opened the door, the sunlight was as bright as I'd ever seen it. As I stepped outside, I felt the heat press down on me. Temperatures had risen in Anatolia, and I knew there was still a long way to travel. I took a breath and held my hand up to block the burning light, and eventually my vision adjusted to the sight of the city.

The Turks were being rounded up by Alexios's forces. They were tied at the hands and shoved through the front gates, dozens at a time. Meanwhile, other guards collected the discarded weapons that littered the ground and dragged away the bloody corpses of the resisters. The Christian citizens were taken care of, guided back to their homes and given supplies. All in all, the battered city had been coldly cleansed. The knights called it a victory, but I felt defeated. The buildings, at least, offered the comfort of familiarity. Alexios had mentioned this was originally part of his empire, so it made sense that I was reminded of Constantinople.

Across the way, there was even a church. Raymond stood at the doors with his hands in prayer and his head down. I made my way towards him and narrowly avoided a group of knights who had charged along the street in celebration. I passed by the abandoned shops and another religious structure – a mosque – that was also empty and silent. I'd never seen one in person.

Raymond sensed me. He raised his head and opened his eyes. Without a word, he flicked his head towards the church. I followed him inside and we sat at a back pew.

Eventually, a priest approached the front podium and began a mass for the many faithful here. His voice was drowned out by Raymond's.

"That armor weighing you down?"

"It's not pleasant, but I think I can manage."

"Good. Julien… just so you're aware, I didn't know they left you with that girl until today."

"Huh? After the battle, you mean?"

"Yes. There was a lot of commotion after you fell unconscious. I had to keep my men in check. Alexios was the one who let the girl tend to your wounds."

"You didn't trust her, sir?"

"No. That's why I asked Adhemar to stay with you."

"Sabuhi seemed all right to me…"

Raymond sniffed and adjusted his jaw. Suddenly I felt nervous.

"That girl might've smiled, might've shown a care – but she could've stuck you with a dagger. Why wouldn't she? We're the infidel – and we just took over her home."

"I – that's not the sense I got from her."

"Sense doesn't matter. Truth does – and what I've said is the truth."

My heart beat faster, and it matched the pain that throbbed in my shoulder.

"Why are you here, Julien?" Raymond turned to face me fully as the wood creaked.

I was frozen.

"Focus." He narrowed his eyes. "Why did you join this war?"

"I want to find my father. But I have the same reason as you – to fight for what I believe in."

"So you believe what I do?" He leaned in slightly. "That there is one God, one faith, one truth – and that we are here to eradicate evil in God's name?"

"I… I do, sir."

"Well you better man up and show me, then!" We spoke low, but his last words were sharp and heavy. The people in front of us turned back with concerned glances. Raymond waved them off and leaned even closer. "I saw the other girl – the survivor – out in the battle."

My head recoiled and my heart pounded out of my chest. I looked away.

"You know what that means, don't you? That tells me those little survivors you let go had the guts to come back and fight us. They could've killed some of our men." Raymond grabbed my collar. "You look at me, boy."

Hesitantly, I met his eyes.

"You must own up to that responsibility, god damn it. You took that on your shoulders like a man, and I expect you to act like one. I can't prove that all of those survivors were there – but you better believe that I'm a breath away from holding you responsible for some of our men dying."

"I'm sorry, sir…"

"Don't be sorry. Stand tall and proud – stand for God. Because this – all of this doubt, all of this questioning and second-guessing what's right – it'll get someone killed. It will cost you everything, and Julien, I'll not have your blood on my hands." He pressed a fist into my chest. "But you won't have this army's blood on yours. Are we clear?"

I took a big, heavy breath. After I reflected, I found myself swayed by my mentor's words. He was right. My doubts had put men at risk. There was one thing I did believe: there was God, and faith, and then there was everything else. If this mission was part of God's will – I had to trust Him.

I looked into Raymond's eyes and said, "We're clear."

Raymond nodded and we returned our attention to the mass. When I prayed, I asked for clarity, for peace of mind, and for strength. I had still wanted things to be easy – black and white.

Outside, our forces continued the exile of the Turks, and I wondered where they would go. Raymond and I headed back towards the front gates.

"Julien, while we're being truthful – I thought I should tell you one more thing."

"Yes?" The bustle of the city quieted in my mind.

"Your father, John. It's time for you let him go."

I stopped, and Raymond continued another few feet before he turned back. "Why?" I barked.

"It should be clear by now."

I lunged forward and grabbed Raymond. He was unfazed. "How can you say that?"

"You saw the bodies on our approach to the city." He paused. "I'm sorry. Let me find a better way to say this…"

I shook my head and dropped to my knees.

Raymond pulled me up by my good arm. "You must stand, Julien."

I looked up at him. "I came here to help my father. To save him."

"God's plan is often not what we expect." Raymond wrapped his arms around me. "But there is something good in all of this, Julien. John gave everything for God. He died for Him – so that means your father is right by His side."

I held onto Raymond tightly. "But I want to see him again."

"You will, in time. And the beauty is, for what we're doing on this journey, we will be welcomed to heaven just the same. We will be right by the Lord's side too."

I stepped back. "You think so?"

"Look in your heart. I know it, and you do too. For now, we must carry on – for God and for your father."

I let out a shaky, emotional breath. I'd ignored it, dreaded it, and kept it in a dark corner of my mind – I didn't want to accept that he was gone. But I had to let my father go. I imagined him in God's arms, and though it didn't make it easier, it was enough to help me move on.

I wiped away the stray tears and said, "I guess we should get back to camp, then."

"Right." Raymond nodded. "Come on."

Back at camp, my mentor allowed me to rest for a while. We were still waiting on the supplies – mainly food – from Alexios. I cried for hours and eventually passed out from exhaustion. When I woke, it was late in the evening, and the torch near my makeshift bed glowed faintly. I sat up with a painful reminder of my injury and headed to see what was going on in camp.

Things were calm. Many soldiers relaxed around campfires and enjoyed dinner. Raymond stood with Adhemar, and I caught the end of a conversation as I approached from the side.

"I'd never want it to happen to him," Raymond said. "It would break my heart. But you understand, don't you? He's—" The knight sensed me again. He turned his head. "Oh, hello Julien."

"Am I interrupting?" I asked. It was an odd feeling – I felt out of place, like I'd walked in on some secret.

"No," Adhemar replied. "I was in the middle of telling Sir Raymond that I expect you to recover stronger than ever. And I was telling him about your heroism in the battle."

"Oh, well, I had your help…"

"Don't even think about being modest," Raymond said with a chuckle. "You were badly wounded, and you kept on fighting. It's something to be proud of."

"I'm just glad you're both safe." I smiled.

"Yes, me too. So, Julien, you've probably seen all the food around camp, yes? We received the supplies."

"Yes, I'm feeling a bit hungry myself."

"You should enjoy a good meal. All of this – it's likely to be the last gift we'll be accepting from Alexios." He sighed as he rubbed his forehead.

"Really? Why?"

"Don't worry about that for now."

"If you say so, sir. When will we be setting out, anyway?"

"Probably in a week. We're just coordinating our next move."

"Hopefully I'll feel better by then."

"Don't push yourself," Adhemar said. "Just focus on recovering."

"Sure. I guess I'll go grab some food." I waved as I left, but I couldn't help feel like they had spoken secrets about me.

I ate alone that night. I tried to get as much rest as possible for the day ahead. The next morning, I woke up in a hot sweat. For the next few days, I watched Raymond's training drills with his knights.

I observed tense duels, horse races, and heated shouting matches over who was better at either. On the fifth day, after a competition escalated to a brawl between two of his knights, Raymond solved their issues and went off on his own. He rested under a tree, his face a vacant stare like he was deep in thought.

That evening, Adhemar summoned me. He wanted to teach me the lay of the land going forward. Up till that point, I'd relied on the army, the trail of humanity before me, to find the way to Jerusalem. It turned out that he had an old map, brown and tattered in a few spots. We sat down together at a small table. He pushed aside some bread crumbs and laid the parchment out under the dusk sun.

He slid a finger along what had been the main trail so far, from Constantinople to Nicaea. My eyes followed as he drew down, and then up and past some lines he'd marked. Finally, he drew back down a long way until he hit Jerusalem.

"Well," I said, "if there were no Turks in the way, I might say it seems pretty straightforward."

Adhemar laughed heartily. "As do many things, until we see them for ourselves."

"So what's in store for us? What are the markings you made?"

"Mountains. We'll be going uphill plenty from here on out."

"I see." I leaned forward with my hands on my knees.

"We could take two paths to Jerusalem. One through the mountains, near friendly Christian territory. Or we could go along the coast. That might be easier, as we could be supported from the sea by Alexios." Adhemar paused, and turned his head to look at Raymond. "But I wonder if that'll happen."

"How come?"

"I suspect Sir Raymond will let us know, soon enough. If you can't already tell why he'd refrain from the emperor's help – well, you're more innocent than I figured, Julien." He frowned.

I folded my arms. "I feel like I'm being left out all of a sudden, like... like I'm not trusted. Between this and the conversation you two had a few days ago."

Adhemar sat up straight and glanced away. "Forgive me." His eyes shifted back to meet mine. "Just stay close to us when battle finds us. That's all you have to do. All right?"

"Fine," I grumbled. "I trust you – all right?"

"That means a great deal."

"So what next, then?" I tapped a finger on the map.

"Right. If things go well, we'd end up back along the coast with a straight path to Jerusalem."

"But there must be other barriers." I pointed at another spot. A long, black line.

"Yes. Another Seljuk fortress – Antioch."

"You've seen it?"

"I did. I made this map on my pilgrimage."

"That's amazing. Well... will Antioch be worse than Nicaea?"

"Yes. Its walls span miles... I've never seen anything like it. I fear it will be our greatest hurdle." The knight's eyes were locked on the map. "Of course, this is assuming we can make it there with enough food. And through the heat."

"It must be possible. We've come so far already." I sat back in the chair and stared up to the sky. I heard the parchment crinkle. When I looked back, Adhemar was holding the rolled-up map in front of me.

"Take it," he said. "In case we ever get split up."

"Are you sure? What about you?"

"There are other maps in camp. And if they're wrong, well, I can correct them."

I smiled and accepted the gift. I carefully stored it in my pack. "Thanks. I just pray that God will see us through this. It's meant to be, isn't it?"

He frowned. "I guess we'll see, won't we?"

Chapter 11

As the sun set and a twilight sky lit up our camp, Raymond shot to his feet. He marched in front of a large group of our army.

"My friends!" he cried. All of the knights stood at attention. "I have a message for you! Those who can hear me, pass this along to your neighbors. Make certain everyone in camp knows!" Countless men and women drifted over from the far side of camp. Suddenly, I was pressed in against dozens of people.

"Tomorrow, we march!" Raymond continued. A cheer erupted from the excited army. My mentor was joined by Adhemar and soon, the other leaders made their way to his side. "Alexios tells me we should follow the coast, so he could aid us with ships." He paced back and forth. "Well, my friends, I say no to that. I'm finished being told what to do by a deceiving fool!" Another, more raucous cheer resounded, which sent a vibration through me. "A man who we came to help – who we came to save. And how does he repay us? He sends us to fight for him, to die in battle, only to steal our victory from us!" Raymond tensed a fist. Violent anger was written on his face, and it burned in his eyes. I'd never seen it from him before. It scared me.

My vision became obstructed as another iron-clad man stepped in front of me. I wove through the crowd to see my mentor.

Raymond laughed, exasperated. "No, we will find our own way. It is we and we alone who can claim to be God's army – and we will win this war on our own. Who is with me?" He thrust a fist into the air.

Amidst another mighty cheer, I noticed Adhemar speaking to Raymond. There was no way to hear what was said in the noise. The bishop touched my mentor's arm, but the latter moved away and continued his reckoning.

"I ask again, are you with me, my friends? Let me hear the voices of the faithful!"

The loudest cheer yet resounded. I was silent. I didn't know what to think. I simply wanted to trust Raymond – and that seemed, as of late, a little more difficult.

"We are with you, Sir Raymond!" the towering Bohemond called. "We'll tear the Turks limb from limb. We don't need any help from pompous diplomats!" Tancred, who stood in the shadow of his uncle, smiled from ear-to-ear.

"We've had our differences," Godfrey added, "but I agree with you. We have the greatest army ever assembled – we will cleave through the non-believers!"

Adhemar clasped his hands together. Through the war cries, he prayed. It was when several soldiers called his name that he opened his eyes and answered.

"Your passion is simply stunning. It is both beautiful and terrifying." The energy in the crowd dipped. "But know this – I am with you, every step of the way. I came to fight for the Lord, and that's what I will do." Finally, he raised his voice to a battle cry: "I am with you!"

A final, wild cry erupted from this crowd. It was hard not to be affected, uplifted, pulled into the storm. I found myself charged as well.

"Tonight, let us rest and pray!" Raymond concluded. "Gather your strength, your arms, and your will. Tomorrow, we set out!"

For the rest of the evening, I was anxious and nauseous, and I stayed awake deep into the night. It was Adhemar who helped me calm down. He comforted me just by being near. Before we separated to go to bed, he said one last thing to me.

"No matter what happens, no matter how dark it may seem, know that the Lord is smiling on you."

And then, it was morning. It was another hot day with the sun pressing down on us. I scrambled to get my equipment on, as did many other soldiers nearby. The leaders were already prepared. They stood near the gates of Nicaea in the distance. Raymond's armor shone, as did Bohemond and Tancred's dark iron, Adhemar's chainmail, and even Godfrey's heavy knight's gear.

I took one more walk through Nicaea with Raymond to reflect on my first battle. It was eerie how empty the streets were for a city of this size. There was still a tension in the air, like the energy of the battle hadn't dissipated yet. I was unsettled by the dark red stains in the dirt and the stray bows and swords still scattered throughout the city.

Many Christian citizens were inside their homes, likely still in shock from the battle. The church, at least, was occupied, and hopeful hymns echoed out. The mosque remained quiet, as if it was frozen in time. Shadows moved inside. A woman emerged, with gray hair that peeked out from her hijab. She peered at me, and a tremendous sadness passed to me. I didn't know what had happened, but Raymond sensed something was wrong.

"Julien," he firmly said. I snapped to attention. "What's the matter? You look sick – is your injury bothering you?"

"No, sir. I just… that woman over there… I wonder if someone she knew was a victim of the battle." My eyes remained locked on hers.

Raymond moved in front of me, blocking my view. "Stop looking at her like that."

I swallowed hard. "What do you mean?"

"Those are the eyes of sympathy. Don't you get it?" He suddenly slapped me, and the jolt of pain reverberated through my face. "Are you listening to me?"

"Sir, I… I'm sorry."

"Stop apologizing!" He smacked me again. "Either you are here to kill, to destroy, or you're not. That is our mission, our duty!" He pointed behind him. "That woman – these people – they are not our friends. We are here to slaughter them for God – nothing else! The only reason she's even standing there is because Alexios is weak. Can you not see the truth, Julien? These are your enemies. To deny that is to deny your faith."

"I… I understand," I meekly replied as I rubbed my cheek. "But they… they are people, aren't they?"

Raymond shook his head and looked down at me with disappointment. It hurt me much more than his physical blows. "I can only give you one chance, one choice to make, Julien."

I stood up straight.

"Either you decide to see the truth and do your duty, or you don't. If you second guess yourself and stray from your faith… it will be your downfall." He paused, and a terrible feeling latched onto me.

120

I slowly nodded. Raymond knelt in front of me, and his tone became much gentler. "Julien… I care about you. I want you to see this war through – with me. You'll do it, won't you?"

"Yes," I managed to say. I half-smiled. "I care about you too, sir. And I want that as well."

"Good." He smiled. "Then let's do it. Trust in God – all else will follow."

I calmed down eventually, and the two of us returned to camp.

Alexios was there, and he saw our army off with a wave, but it appeared more like he was shooing them.

With that, we were ready to leave. Adhemar brought our horses over.

He looked at me intently. "Your cheek is bruised," he said. "Are you all right?"

"Oh," I replied, and touched my face. "Yes, I'm fine." I offered him a false smile.

I think he saw through my lie, but he didn't press me. He patted my Arabian horse a few times, and we both saddled up. "Have you decided on a name for her yet?"

"No, not yet. I haven't had time to really think in a while." I gave my white horse a good pat. "Sorry, girl. Bear with me. I'll find the perfect name for you."

We met up with Raymond at the front of the army and continued along the well-trod path used by the Byzantines, Turks, and pilgrims alike. The sound of the army hadn't changed from the start of my journey. It had always been the low rumble of thunder behind us, a drum that pushed us forward.

The excitement for what was next tapered off after a few days of travel. Far worse, though, was what Adhemar had warned me about: the heat of Anatolia became a serious issue. We'd just entered the summer month of June, and with over twenty pounds of armor on my injured body, the days were like a glimpse of hell. We had water, but there was hardly any cover from the sun on the hilly trail. The evenings, at least, offered some mercy where we could take cover in the shade and slightly cooler temperatures.

On the fourth day of sweltering travel, the leaders met at the front of our forces to discuss how to proceed. I listened in closely.

"This will be too difficult for one group," Raymond said. "We're going to need to find food in the area eventually – we should split our forces to make that easier."

"Agreed," Adhemar replied. "Half of us tearing through the land is better than the whole bunch. How shall we split up?"

"I'll take my nephew," Bohemond muttered. "The two of us will suffice with our troops. Don't worry about us."

"Are you certain? Your forces are considerable, but..."

"You doubt us, Adhemar? I said don't worry – so don't. We'll meet up outside Dorylaeum. It's not much farther now. We'll regroup there with whatever supplies we can find."

"I trust you, Sir Bohemond. If you think that's best, then we'll do that. Godfrey?"

The Frenchman scoffed. "I don't care. Do what you wish."

"Then it's settled," the giant grumbled. "We'll go on ahead."

The two broke off along another trail, and the stream of their Italian soldiers followed. I couldn't guess how many troops they had. It numbered in the thousands at least, and according to Adhemar, made up about half of our total forces. Even so, I felt vulnerable.

From there, we trudged for several hours. We foraged nearby. I joined Adhemar and a collection of knights for that brief detour to make sure supplies remained high. Back on the trail, a group of horses raced down a hill on our left. I whipped my head over. I'd expected an attack, but it was allies.

"Help!" the lead soldier shouted. The others were just as frantic. "Please, we need you!"

"What's happened?" Raymond cried as he charged up to them on horseback.

"It's the Turks – we were attacked near Dorylaeum! We'll be slaughtered unless you hurry!"

"Right, soldier!" Raymond raised his voice to a battle cry. "Hear that, men? We're off to slay some Turks! With me!"

"Aye!" I shouted, in time with a massive cheer behind me.

A frenzied rush along the trail slowly fell into an exhausted walk as neither we nor our horses could sustain the pace. We were farther away from Bohemond than we expected. Hills soon turned into a claustrophobic valley.

After several excruciating minutes, we heard the sounds of battle echo in the distance. My horse's hooves clicked through the wet grass as the ground turned marshy. Finally, we saw Bohemond's camp being pelted with arrows. Bodies littered my view, both ours and our enemies. The Italian knights were grouped up with their shields held high, but many of their horses had been victims of the volleys. The Turks' numbers were shocking to me, especially after their defeat at Nicaea. I saw no end to them.

Raymond guided us away from a straight-on approach. We joined the battle from the side, but we swept around through some trees and cut behind the enemy as they besieged the knights' camp. The Turks hadn't noticed us yet. The trees and shade had masked us. Adhemar and Raymond thrust their silver swords to the sky.

"Charge!" they yelled in tandem.

My ears were rocked by the army's mighty response, though I

was right there with them. Together with Raymond and Adhemar and the massive army behind us, we charged.

This time, I had to let go of my fear. This time... I believed I had to kill.

The Turks were taken by surprise, their faces marked with it. Most wheeled away on their horses, but our charge gave them little time to think. We fell upon them in a flash.

In the fray, I clashed swords with an enemy on horseback. I tried to knock his weapon away, but he disengaged. I chased after him as Raymond cut down an enemy to my left. I heard Adhemar rally the troops, and that gave me a surge of energy. Another Turk shot an arrow at me that barely whizzed by my helmet. I spun my horse and pursued the new target. I heard Raymond shout behind me, accompanied by a separate scream of death as he killed my original foe.

It was complete chaos. I staggered from enemy to enemy, barely able to keep focused and stay near my allies. The Turks sent a huge volley of arrows our way, which cut down another groups who screamed as they fell.

After frantic minutes of battle, a Turk charged right up to me with rage in his eyes. I blocked his quick strike and slashed his chest. Blood spurted from his torn clothes, and he cried out in pain. He pressed a hand to his wound. I was locked in the frenzy of battle, of pure survival – I slashed him again. This time, he toppled off his horse and slowly, he died. I'd secured my first kill – it was a surreal, electric, and miserable feeling.

I kept on fighting, but I had been drawn away from the main battle. I turned back at one point and saw Raymond. He stared at me coldly.

I hadn't realized my separation from my allies until it was too

124

late. I breathed heavily, and my mind raced much too quickly to keep up with everything around me. It was one big blur.

It was at the moment when I was most confused, most uncertain what to do next, in a line of trees where my sense of direction was mixed up, when I was struck in the side by an enemy's weapon. I flew off my horse and slammed into the ground. I gasped for air. I thought I was dying. But I wasn't cut, I wasn't bleeding. At least I didn't think so. After a fearful few seconds, my breathing returned. The sounds of battle were distant. I angled my head left, and I saw my horse. To my surprise, she hadn't run away. I looked right and saw the legs of dozens of the Turks' black horses. It sent a chill of abject fear through me.

One of them hopped off horseback, and his dark outfit draped down in the dirt. He knelt beside me.

It was Ahtmar. He looked at me with his black, fiery eyes, which pierced my very soul.

I desperately reached for my sword and grabbed it from the grass beside me. As I lifted my arm, he kicked my blade away from me. He grabbed my uninjured arm and dragged me up to my feet. Another thunderous noise filled my ears as more horses approached. I barely held my head up from the pain, but I saw the shapes of a hundred more horses.

"What's this?" came a heavy, coarse voice.

"Sultan!" Ahtmar replied.

"You captured this boy? Good for you."

"Yes. He's not like the others, but... he remains an enemy."

"What's your name?"

"Ahtmar, sir. Ahtmar Naji. I don't mean to distract you from the battle, but I wanted to ask about Nicaea..."

"Yes... I'm sorry, Ahtmar. I tried to fight, to defend our home, but I failed. Let us take the fight to them this time, shall we?"

"Yes, sir!"

"First, let us see if we can deter the Franks from battle."

Ahtmar's allies followed as he brought me to the end of the tree line. We could see the fierce battle still underway. I couldn't fight to free myself. The pain in my shoulder had drained all of my strength away.

"Hear me, Franks!" Ahtmar shouted, his voiced booming out to the distance. I saw Raymond and Adhemar. They didn't stop fighting at first, but Raymond eventually saw where the voice came from – and he saw me.

The battle seemed to stop in time as my mentor stared at me.

"You listen to me!" Ahtmar continued in a rage, "I'm going to end this boy's life if you don't surrender!" I felt the sword beside my neck. Ahtmar recognized that Raymond was a leader – my leader. But he didn't realize that Raymond couldn't understand him. A priest quickly scurried behind the knights to translate.

My mentor looked away with pain and anger etched on his face.

"What will it be?" Ahtmar said. He pressed the edge on my neck, and I winced.

Raymond looked at me intently. "Julien... I am sorry, my boy. Truly, I knew this would happen... the Lord has decided your fate. Your mercy and hesitation has cost us lives, and that will send you to the afterlife earlier than it should have. Julien... I pray that you are forgiven."

Adhemar took to his side. He avoided my eyes.

I was stunned. It felt like my heart stopped.

"Men, keep on fighting!" Raymond called. "No remorse!"

With those words, what would happen next seemed inevitable. I expected a sharp pain, and ultimately, I expected this to be my last minute alive.

"Only fitting for you monsters," Ahtmar muttered. He pulled his blade back and smashed me in the head with the hilt. I fell into the blackness of unconsciousness once again.

When I came to, my vision was a blurry haze and my ears were ringing. My senses returned gradually, and I found myself across from Ahtmar in an unfamiliar tent. I couldn't move my arms. I was tied up. Ahtmar sat next to a table, facing away from me, where his bloody sword lay next to a candle that had all but melted to wax. It was dark, but I saw that he had his head in his hands. He was crying.

Even though I was trapped, even though my life could end at any moment, I felt something I hadn't expected: sympathy.

Chapter 12
Three miles outside of Dorylaeum

Ahtmar hadn't seen that I was awake. He continued to quietly weep in the darkness of the tent. I realized then that his forces had almost certainly lost the last battle.

Soon after, a light pierced through the dark in a bright beam. The tent flap opened, and someone stepped inside. It was Zahra. Her presence startled her brother, who hadn't noticed her either. She sat beside him and placed her hands on his shoulders.

"Ahtmar," Zahra tenderly said, "you need to rest."

"I can't," he quietly replied. "Every time I close my eyes, I see our home. I see our people dying."

"I know." She caressed her brother's arm, which reminded me of the terrible pain in mine. "But we overheard what the Christians said at Nicaea. They planned to show mercy to the citizens, and it wasn't those westerners — those Franks — who said that. It was the Byzantines. They have been more generous to us."

"Right, that's true…"

"Do you want to go back home?"

"I do. But it would take more than our small group to deliver justice. We have to reunite with the army."

Zahra hugged her brother. Even in the dark, I felt the girl's care, her warmth, for her sibling. "You must have faith that Allah is working things out for us," she said with a gentle smile. "So, you should rest and let me watch over Julien."

"No." Ahtmar sat up straight. "He's my responsibility."

"All right." She patted his arm softly. "In that case, let me know when he wakes up."

He nodded and his sister returned outside. His head fell into his hands again. I shifted in my chair to relieve my strain. The chair creaked, and the Turk stirred. He glared at me. Then, he brought his chair closer to me. Zahra came back inside. Strangely, my first thought was, I don't want Zahra to see what her brother is about to do to me.

"He's awake?" Zahra said. She leaned over to check on me, and suddenly, embarrassment and anxiety flooded my senses along with my pain.

"I didn't expect to see you again, miss," I stuttered.

"I have a name. It's Zahra."

"Right… Zahra."

"Sister," Ahtmar muttered, "help me understand. I want to talk to him."

"Okay, brother."

"So," the imposing Turk began, "Julien." I nervously adjusted myself in my seat. "Your friends were willing to let you die."

I had no words. I weakly struggled to get free.

"I watched your army approach Dorylaeum. I was surprised to find you at the front of the pack. Seems you found an impressive role for yourself. You and that Raymond." Ahtmar grabbed his crimson-stained sword from the table. "Were you two close? I guess it doesn't matter now."

I exhaled a worried breath. Zahra touched her brother's arm and shook her head. He moved away from her.

"Some of your men looked at you like you were a dog," he continued. "Like they'd push you off a cliff if no one was looking. They'll never forgive you for letting us live."

"Why haven't you killed me?" I barked.

"I should. But you're alive because you have something of a guardian angel. A person this world doesn't deserve."

I yanked my hands down, and pain jolted through my whole body. "If this is some elaborate trick to try and torture me," I said through terrible strain, "can you spare me from it? At least give me a chance to fight for my life."

"I want you to listen. There's another reason you live." The Turk stared at Zahra for a moment, frowned, and then turned back to me. "I told myself that I was going ignore that guardian angel, and fight back your merciless army with a streak of my own cruelty." He paused, and a shiver ran through me. "But then you were abandoned by those you trusted, those you placed your faith in. And that was when I realized: it was a sign from Allah. A sign that I must save a fallen boy, and bring him the light of truth."

"What are you talking about?" I cried. "I'm no boy. You're no older than me."

Ahtmar smiled slightly. His eyes gleamed with knowledge, as though he was 50 years older than me.

His sister looked at him intently. "You're pale, Ahtmar. Are you feeling any better?"

He whispered something to her. I couldn't hear what they said.

"Ah, yes. I understand. Well... do you think you'll go through with the plan? You were in here for a long time deciding."

"Yes... I think so." The Turk gripped his sword a little tighter.

Zahra smiled brightly at him. It almost distracted me from my impending death.

Ahtmar sighed and pushed up to his feet. I studied Zahra as the hopelessness set in. My head dropped and I stared at the shadowed grass.

"I don't understand how we got here," I said. "I might like a chance to learn. But if not – make it quick for me."

I heard the sword as it whooshed through the air, and my whole body tensed up. But then, I felt my arms fall safely into my lap. I stared at my hands and wiggled my fingers. Then, my eyes widened and I gasped.

"Things are not what I expected either," Ahtmar said. "I want you to come along with us."

"Why...?" I weakly replied.

"It is more than what I told you, Julien. Don't you want justice? Don't you want to question your leaders?"

"I..." I tensed my hands. "I don't know. I don't know what to do anymore."

"Would you rather die?"

"No, I just... I need a moment. Please – grant me that."

"Fine. You can run if you want – but there's nowhere to go."

I nodded slowly as my mind went blank.

Ahtmar grabbed my sword. I think he noted the craftsmanship as he flipped it to both sides, and then sheathed the weapon. He exited the tent, and Zahra lingered for just a moment to look at me before she followed her brother into the humid night.

I struggled to my feet. My knees buckled, and I slammed into the ground with a groan. I pushed myself up, and I settled on a knee.

I couldn't think straight, so I observed the Turks' camp through the tent flap.

They had several other tents set up with a crackling campfire in the center of them. I counted 16 of their members who were grouped all around it. I'd instinctively harkened back to Raymond's training on tactics. As his name settled in my mind, so did the memory that he left me for dead.

In any case, the Turks appeared more sullen than even I had been. Zahra consoled her brother as the boy stared off vacantly into the distance. The others were quiet, and some younger-looking members prodded the fire with sticks or held their knees to their chest. But there were a few, particularly an older Turk with a big grey beard, who stood tall.

"Ahtmar?" he asked, and the young Turk snapped to attention. "You're not listening to us. Please, stay focused."

"Sorry, Hilal." He inhaled and sheathed his sword, and then he equipped mine right beside it on his hip. "We have to stay strong. We have to overcome our last defeat. Our forces were split into pieces during the battle. We must reunite with them."

"But what about the prisoner? He didn't work as a hostage the first time. Should we bring him with us?"

"At this point, I don't think he will be our prisoner."

There was a collective gasp from the camp. I quickly moved back a couple of steps.

Ahtmar plopped down at the campfire with his warriors, while Zahra kneeled in the grass near him. Ahtmar said, "I want all of your opinions about our captive, beyond your surprise. I know – allowing him to join us must seem absurd. But we have co-existed with other faiths before – I lived with Christians in Nicaea." I shook my head in foolish disbelief. "That's not the main reason. This might sound strange, but I…" The boy hesitated, and Zahra reached out to touch him softly. He said, "I had a vision, I think. After I saw those armored monsters turn on the boy. I wonder if God is guiding me to redeem him. To show him the way of our faith."

Ahtmar faced many cold stares from his allies, and I couldn't blame them. Each of the Turks here probably thought I would attack them at the first opportunity.

Truly, though – as astonished as I had been by Ahtmar's proposition, I was even more amazed by his kindness, especially in the middle of a war.

He continued, "Julien's supposed brother-in-faith didn't care about him. He let Julien get pulled into our trap. That Raymond cared more about gutting our brothers."

"You're right," one of his allies said as he rubbed his stubbly chin. "You know, Julien doesn't seem much older than me. I guess I don't understand why he was fighting. It didn't seem natural to him. He was stumbling around on his horse and flailing with his sword. Did he even land a blow on any of us?"

I was embarrassed by the combat critique, right as it was, but I was also thankful that they hadn't seen my first regretful kill.

Ahtmar folded my arms. "Do you agree with letting him join us, Bekir?"

"I don't know, my friend. But I will follow you as I always have. Your decision will fly."

Another man stood –the largest and most intimidating of the bunch. He cast a long shadow over the camp. "I have followed you for a while, Ahtmar. I believe you to be a good leader, but I cannot stand for this. I cannot imagine riding alongside one of the butchers who hunt us even as we speak."

Ahtmar stood to meet his challenge. "I will take responsibility for Julien." The large man looked away and tightened his lips. Ahtmar added, "I'll grant you this, Aazim — you can be the first to cut Julien down if he shows signs of rebellion."

After a tense moment, Aazim sat down.

"Ahtmar," the elder Hilal said. "I believe in you." He moved over to the boy and wrapped an arm around his shoulder. "From the moment we began your training, I prayed you would be the Seljuks champion." A gust of wind sailed through the camp, and the flames flickered. "That might not happen, not in the way I originally thought. But you remain courageous and passionate — you are our fire." He sighed. "With you as our leader, I know we can fend off these invaders."

"Thank you," Ahtmar replied as he bowed his head. "What about Julien?"

"I support your decisions. I will leave it at that." The elder Turk smiled and rejoined the campfire.

"I would like to use the boy as a hostage again," another Turk said. This man had been quiet until now, but as soon as he spoke, his large presence was felt. "We couldn't convince Raymond, but there surely must be others within the enemy ranks that would negotiate to save a child."

"You think so?" Ahtmar sadly said.

Emotion took hold of me. Both from Ahtmar's tone, and when I'd thought of that potential other person the Turk wondered about — I believed it would have been Adhemar. But even the pope's bishop hadn't helped me when it mattered most.

Ultimately, Ahtmar said, "I won't use Julien that way, Naasir. It's wrong. It's against the teachings of God. And it would serve no purpose. We have nothing that needs doing except battle. Would we not have a more effective warrior if we welcomed an ally instead

135

of a tool?"

Much of this brotherhood of Turks was quiet. Eventually, after some deliberation, and through my terrible pain and nerves, everyone came to an agreement: I would live, and join them.

Of course, it seemed I had no say in this. Then again, I really had no idea what I would've said.

I needed to face this challenge, rather than endure the endless struggle within myself. I removed my armor, slowly, painfully, which left me in my plain tunic and pants. I felt lighter, and not just from the pounds of iron lifted from my shoulders.

At the end of the Turks' discussion, one other younger member, who I would later learn was called Sami, had a message for his leader.

"You're our only hope, Ahtmar. I believe we would've been wiped out already without your help. I don't know if I can do it happily, or easily, but I'll try and welcome Julien."

"I appreciate your honesty," Ahtmar replied. "It's settled then."

"That just leaves one mystery," Hilal muttered. "The goal of our enemy's massive army."

"Yes. I know it isn't simply a military effort. They had women and children in their camp at the last battle. Whatever they're doing, it's a mass movement of all sorts of people."

I finally worked up my courage. I opened the tent flap and stepped out into the light. I was faced with over a dozen bows aimed at me. The Turkish brotherhood was ready to put me down if need be. I simply stared ahead. I tried to lift my hands up, but I couldn't.

"Hold your fire!" Ahtmar shouted. The Turks stood down. Zahra – and Hilal – were ready to relay my Latin words to their leader, but I tried to speak Arabic as best I could.

"I can tell you what they're after. I don't know how it came to this, but... I will tell you everything I know."

"We're listening," Ahtmar nodded.

The brush rustled behind him. Zahra walked behind one of the tents. When she came back into view, she led my white horse towards me. I looked on in amazement.

"I hope this shows you we mean well," Zahra said as she petted the horse. "She's beautiful, by the way. Have you got a name for her?"

I hesitated for a moment. "Thank you... Oh, no, I haven't decided on a name yet."

"You'll find one eventually." She smiled and returned to her brother's side. "Please continue, Julien."

"Right." I swallowed hard. "My army... they want Jerusalem. They want to free it from your – from the Seljuks control."

My captors looked at one another, shocked.

"So that's it," the new leader said. "But this is obviously more than a military campaign. What kind of picture does your army have of Jerusalem?"

"It's terrible. We were told Christians were being killed and enslaved under your rule... We were sent to rescue them."

"That doesn't make sense," Naasir chimed in. "My family lives there, and I've been there often. The Christians are not under our heels. They have their own quarter, and they are respected."

I raised a hand to my forehead. "I don't know what to think anymore. That picture was painted by a person who I put my faith in. But... as soon as I arrived here from the west... things became unclear."

"You're thinking for yourself," Zahra said. "For a long time, my brother and I saw things plainly too. That's what our leaders tell us to do, but you've seen that it's not as simple as that."

"Let me ask you something, Julien," Ahtmar said. "If you could return to your army... would you?"

"I want to see them again," I quietly said.

The boy bore down on me. "You should know something, then. I would never let you go back if you plan on bringing more death to my brothers."

I looked at him intently. "If I returned, I would talk to Raymond. I would see if we could reach an understanding with your people."

"That's not going to happen. You must see that already."

I nodded slowly a few times.

Ahtmar smiled grimly. "You're welcome to try." He turned to the other Turks. "Anyway, we should get moving."

With nods of approval from his allies, he moved to the tent where I'd been held to grab my things. He was taken aback by how heavy my armor was, but he seemed to admire the craftsmanship of my shield as he ran a hand across it. Then he tossed everything outside into the grass and disassembled the tent.

The rest of the Turks followed his lead, and they took down the camp quickly. I was lost. I didn't know whether to run away, lash out in anger, or help them.

Once Ahtmar had stamped out the campfire, Zahra checked on him. They hugged, and then the brother turned to me. "I gave you a choice – either join us or die. Do you want answers?"

"I do," I replied.

"Then get your things together. Are you going to take that unwieldy armor?"

"Yes… I think so."

They all watched me put on my equipment, piece by piece. To them, it must have been like a foreign ceremony. I'm sure our bulky iron defense must have seemed unnecessary to their swift, elegant tactics.

In any case, my body ached with the armor back on. Finally, I held up my coat, and stared at the crimson cross. I frowned.

I think, in that moment, I'd realized what I needed to do to find guidance. I put on the coat, and then hoisted my shield on my back.

"My weapon?" I meekly asked Ahtmar.

"No." He tapped it as it rested on his hip alongside his curved sword.

He paced towards our group of horses, and then held his arms out to the side. "The truth is, no one knows what will happen next. We'll have to find out together."

I hopped on my horse. The Turks trained their bows on me again. "I can't believe I'm saying this," I muttered, "but I agree." Ahtmar had his allies stand down, and I moved up next to him. "I know I have no right to suggest this, but… I wish to go to the holy land."

Ahtmar half-smiled. "Is that so?" He stared out at the horizon, at the forest, hills, and the trail that – eventually – led to Jerusalem. "Maybe that's not a bad idea."

Zahra hopped onto her brother's horse and latched onto him. "I want to go, too. It might offer clarity."

The brotherhood took to their horses. Naasir rode up next to us.

"If we go," he said, "I'd have connections with my family. Getting into the city shouldn't be a problem."

"All right," Ahtmar said. Suddenly, he seemed energized. A smile crept across his face, and he sat up straight.

Maybe my suggestion had been the right one, and not just for me. The holy land was sacred to so many people in the world, and that included the Turks.

Ahtmar said, "First, we have to find more of our forces – and catch up to the Franks. I can guess where they're going next, but I want to hear it from you, Julien."

I squeezed my reigns. "They mentioned another fortress city – Antioch."

"Yes… of course. All right then – that's our next destination. Let's go!"

The brotherhood stormed off into the blazing day, and somehow, against everything I'd ever believed, I was right there with them.

On the road, we kept a blistering pace towards Antioch, and mustered as much travel as we could in the heat. It lasted through the day, and we made camp for the night.

I was by myself as Ahtmar and his allies cooked dinner around the campfire. I lay back against a tree and looked out towards a bright, starry sky. Silently, I questioned the heavens.

The brotherhood eyed me with suspicion throughout the night. Understandable as it was, it didn't make it any easier for me to rest my injured body, let alone my mind. But as I looked past the fiery eyes of the Turks, I saw Zahra. The girl stared at me sadly instead.

She spoke to her brother, but I couldn't hear their words from where I sat. Shortly after, they brought me dinner – together. My thanks were a whisper, and I struggled to hold back my tears. I still couldn't believe what I'd lost, and where I'd found myself.

That night, I had terrible nightmares about my former friends. I relived their massacres, and my part in them, and I stared at their backs as they walked away from me forever.

The next week was composed mainly of sweltering days and uneasy, distant nights. Each evening, though, the siblings brought me food. I hadn't realized it until later, but with each meal, Zahra moved a little closer to me. And each time, she stayed a little longer. My dark dreams persisted, but they were just a little lighter

– enough to carry me onwards.

The following morning, we faced a problem on our path forward: much of the terrain had been burned. I had no idea what could've happened, but it was Ahtmar who revealed the truth as he glared at me:

"My people wanted to deprive your army of food." He glanced away, and his next words were much softer. "Is it that dire...?"

Despite the trail of cinders, we did well on supplies. Caring for a group of 17 had certainly been easier than the mass of humanity we chased. We foraged to keep supplies steady and, hesitantly, I helped them as best I could.

We journeyed a few hazier, heat-washed summer weeks. Along the way, I kept to my lessons. I tried to learn more Arabic words to aid in my survival.

As the reality of my situation set in, and I couldn't pretend I was in some impossible dream, something finally sunk in about the Turks: they prayed, too.

Where my prayers were often silent and brief, the Turks had an elegant ritual. It was something they repeated, often five times in a day. And truly, even to my naïve, foolish eyes, it was beautiful to behold.

They prayed in unison, in symmetry, and in true humble piety. They cleaned themselves before prayer, which was something I'd never even considered doing before. They spoke quiet words, honored God, and bowed in service to Him.

The first time I saw it, I was astonished – nearly breathless. After a while, it became something I looked forward to seeing – it was that beautiful to me. And eventually, from a distance, I joined in their prayers with my own.

I thought about what Raymond would have said if he was

here. How angry he would have been by my respect for the Turks' prayers. But by then, I'd realized that my mentor couldn't see what I could. The Turks were believers, too, but somewhere along the way, we'd diverged as people. I wasn't wise enough to determine why, but I did know prayer when I saw it – and I knew it was honest, true, and full of undeniable love.

I aspired to carry that love with me – otherwise, I didn't think I'd survive my journey.

———————

The Turks and I shared other similarities. For one, Ahtmar experienced his own nightmares. He had his own tent which he shared with his sister, but even as I rested a distance away, I heard his desperate cries during my own sleepless nights.

Zahra didn't fare better, which broke my heart.

One night, Ahtmar sat atop a large rock while he was on guard duty. He had been looking at me when I heard his sister talking in his tent.

Hilal walked up to him. "You should check on her," he said. As Ahtmar glanced towards the elder Turk, I couldn't help but move closer. Hilal spoke more quietly, but I heard him add, "And honestly, you should rest more. You have no color in your face. You haven't for quite some time now."

Ahtmar slid down the rock to his feet, and I stumbled back. "I can hardly sleep. But thank you. I'll check on Zahra."

He paced up to his tent, peeked through, and then stepped inside. I simply sat down and listened.

"No!" Zahra screamed. "Leave us alone!"

I felt a twinge in my heart. I heard the girl awaken startled, with quick, frantic breaths that came through muffled outside the tent.

"Oh, Ahtmar," she said shakily. "What's going on?"

"You were just having a bad dream – I couldn't let it go on. I'm sorry to wake you."

"Oh… that's fine. Thank you."

"Was it about Nicaea?"

She didn't answer, but I knew the truth. Anyone would.

As our travel continued, we couldn't seem to catch up to my army. Eventually, we came to a split in the road. An imposing mountain loomed far in the distance. Naasir seemed to recognize it. He waved Ahtmar over, while I pulled out the map out from my pack.

"Ahtmar," Naasir began, "those are the Taurus Mountains. We have to decide on which road to take."

The Turk leader glanced at me. "Do you know which way your army went?"

"I have a guess," I said. "Sorry, um… Naasir, was it?" The bushy-bearded Turk grinned and nodded. "I was under the impression we could go through the mountains, or along the coast. Is that right?"

"Correct," Naasir said. "The coast would be faster."

"I believe that my allies went up into the mountains. I'd heard there was friendly territory that way."

"Armenia. That would hold true. It's Christian territory."

"So what do we do, Ahtmar?" Aazim asked. "Do we trust the boy?"

"He wouldn't be able to know for certain," Zahra replied. "He was with us, wasn't he? He wouldn't have seen which way they went. If you're thinking he's lying, well, he could be wrong even if he did." Aazim trotted away, and cursed under his breath.

"I understand if you don't want to trust me," I said. "But my allies didn't want to accept Byzantine help, which would've come by the coast. That's another reason they intended to turn away from the sea."

143

"I trust you," Zahra said.

"Oh, well… thank you!"

"Well," Bekir said, "seems to me that in both cases, it's faster to go by the coast. I say we do that."

"Agreed," Hilal added.

"All right," Ahtmar said. "Let's go."

Our journey continued down the winding path, towards the sea. I had no idea if we could reach Antioch before my frenzied allies did, but deep down, I knew I was headed for another massacre.

Chapter 13
Several days later

I felt alone for quite some time. I lost track of the days. Somewhere in the swirling chaos of emotions, I turned seventeen. But what's a birthday when you feel like you're by yourself?

Things on my journey weren't simple. I realized that more quickly than I ever expected. God's plan had been murky and dark, and it had grown more uncertain by the day. Or maybe it had become clearer.

I still held onto a glimmer of hope: I would be welcomed back into the French army. Raymond would rush out to save me. This journey was some illusion I'd created in the hazy, blazing summer.

But the sun still beamed above me. The sweat still trickled down my skin. I was face-to-face with reality, and that knowledge made me ask if I really wanted to reunite with them. My allies rejected me and left me behind simply for choosing one of the most important qualities of my faith: kindness.

In my last conversation with Raymond, I had told him I understood his motivations – his goals – to kill and destroy. But I hadn't. My doubts nested within me. Some days, I felt paralyzed.

There was only one thing that made it possible to push on. One person, who had been surrounded by flames, scarred by a war's hatred, and still carried a light within her. The light that I almost couldn't recognize anymore.

Zahra.

Antioch was a few days ahead of us. We made camp right near the sea. I welcomed the misty breeze, and the bright stars that lit up the water. I closed my study book and tucked it away, lay back in the grass with my hands behind my head.

It was quiet. Most of Ahtmar's brotherhood were asleep. The large Aazim was on watch with three others, and as I peeked back, they glowered at me with fiery, spiteful eyes.

I could've fled to my silver allies – the thought had crossed my mind more than once – but I wanted to see this through. It seemed like I would cross paths with them in any case. They were almost certainly going to Antioch, too.

Just as the water's waves made my eyes feel heavy, Zahra swung into my view from around the tree. She playfully laughed as she startled me. I sat up and wondered for a frantic moment whether I should move away or pretend I was sleeping. But her deep brown eyes, gentle and warm, calmed me down.

"Um, hi, Zahra," I finally said.

"Hello." She took a few steps towards the beach and took off her boots to plant her bare feet on the sand. She turned her head slightly towards me. "I wanted to apologize, Julien."

"Huh? How come?"

"For slapping you."

I rubbed my cheek with a half-smile. "Don't worry. I had it coming."

"No – you were the only one who cared about stopping the killing."

"Thank you, Zahra."

"But I've been meaning to speak with you, anyway. I had to wait for Ahtmar to relax. He wouldn't be happy with me doing this alone. He's finally getting a full night's sleep."

"I suppose I can understand him. He wants to protect you from me."

She faced me. "Do you really mean that?"

"Well… I can see why he would be distrustful of me. I can't say I trust him, either." She frowned. "Not to be disrespectful. It's simply that… none of this is what I expected to happen."

"Same for me. For all of us, really." Her long, blue dress was brushed aside by the wind, and she dug her toes into the sand. "That's why I'm hoping we can learn something from journeying together."

I smiled. "Yeah." A cool breeze washed over me, and I sighed. "I hope so too."

"I meant to ask you – you said before that you went to war to save Jerusalem." Zahra glanced down, and then back to me. "Do you still believe that?"

I stared at the campfire, then refocused on Zahra. "I'm not sure. But what's happened lately has shown me a deeper truth, one that has me asking a lot of questions."

"Well, I'm glad. Was that the only reason why you came?"

"No, actually. I followed after my father, who came here earlier in the war. He's missing – no, he's passed on."

"I see…"

"It's all right," I said with a soft smile. "I appreciate you asking about it. What about your family, aside from Ahtmar?"

"Our parents were sick, and God took them." My heart dropped, and my mouth fell open. It made my own struggle seem small by comparison. The girl noticed my reaction and said, "Don't worry,

Julien. They're safe now. And they didn't have to deal with the war we now face – for that, I'm thankful."

"I'm sorry even so, Zahra," I said, placing a hand over my heart. "You're strong. So very strong. Do you know that?"

Zahra tilted her head and looked at me with curiosity. I might've said she was trying to figure me out. She scrunched up her nose. It was kind of cute. Under the starlight, she really glowed, even if much of her head was covered in her blue shroud. It made me recall something. Suddenly, I felt a little anxious.

"Hey… I was just reminded of something I wanted to say to you."

"What's that?" Zahra moved towards me.

"Do you remember a few weeks ago, when you said my horse was beautiful?" I pointed to my Arabian steed that rested in the nearby grass.

"Yes, sure. What about it?"

"Well, I wanted to say… I thought you were beautiful too." Hopefully the night disguised my flushed cheeks.

Zahra giggled, and leaned forward slightly. "That's sweet."

I got to my feet and brushed some dirt off my clothes. "Thanks." I frowned. "You know, the first time I saw you…" My words trailed off as the nightmare massacre flashed through my mind. "Seeing you like that broke my heart. What we did torments me. I can't undo it, but I suppose I can say… you opened my eyes."

She walked up next to me, and we both looked out towards the sea. "The fact that you're questioning your mission – your beliefs – is something I respect. The others marching through the mountains… they'll bring doom upon my world."

"You're right. Even the people I care for most seem to be deadset on this war."

"Some day, my people will have to fight back. It may be soon, it

148

may not. Either way, that isn't a pleasant thought."

"I agree." I sighed. "Truly, I can hardly make sense of anything right now… but I wonder if we can find clarity together."

I felt her eyes on me. She smiled again. It was a much more welcome sight than our first meeting. "It's worth a try."

"When we get to Antioch, I will talk to my leaders on your behalf."

"Thank you, Julien."

Zahra and I sat on the beach and listened to the waves run along the shore. It didn't last as long as I'd hoped.

I felt the energy first. An oppressive feeling crept up on me. I stirred and made my way to my feet. Zahra must've felt it too. She did the same. When I turned around, four bows were trained on me. That wasn't unusual as of late, but the ill-intent – the killing intent – was.

"Well, look at this," Aazim said with a cold smirk. He lowered his bow and drew a sword. "What are you two up to over here?"

Neither of us said a word. It felt like nothing we could say would help.

He paced back and forth. "And we wonder why Allah has been silent to us." He laughed. "So, what – we're just making friends with the people who are gutting us left and right?"

"Julien is no such person," Zahra firmly said. "He hasn't taken a life – isn't that right, Julien?"

"You've been kind, Zahra. But I won't lie – I killed a Seljuk warrior." The girl quietly gasped. I took a step forward. "But my mind has been changed. I was brought here because of faith – I believed I was right – but is there no room for learning from mistakes?"

"When the mistake is so grave," Aazim replied, "why would we offer forgiveness?"

149

I found a sudden bout of courage. I planted my feet firmly in the sand. "Are you going to strike me down? I have no weapon. I only carry my heart right now. And I'm telling you that I've changed my perspective. I've laid the truth bare."

"Ahtmar is just as pathetic as you." He spat on the ground, and then glared at Zahra. "He's a coward who listens to the whims of a fool girl. You'll both suffer for that, and you'll drag us down to hell with you."

"You're the coward," Zahra growled. "You're happy to say this now, while my brother sleeps."

"He won't be our leader for long." He paused. "When the time is right, we will strike down anyone who stands against us." He narrowed his eyes at Zahra. "Including you, if need be."

My blood boiled, and I moved in front of Zahra. But she was the one who fired back. "You're no rebel. You're a scheming bully. You're not even a man if you won't stand up to my brother."

Aazim's grin grew. He and his group of three headed back to camp. I watched them every step of the way as my heart pounded in anger.

Ahtmar emerged from his tent, behind their campfire. I wondered if it wasn't a coincidence. Maybe he had felt the dangerous energy too. He eyed Aazim, who held his blade out over the campfire, and then Zahra's brother walked towards us.

"Thank you for visiting me," I said to Zahra. "And for everything you've said." She nodded at me with a gentle smile. My next words flowed from my soul, "I promise I will do everything I can to stop this war."

With that, I hurried towards a tree on a nearby hill. From there, I watched the siblings. Ahtmar hugged and doted over his sister. He franticly pointed in my direction, and Zahra shook her head. Her

150

brother then listened as she leaned in to whisper to him. Aazim was watching, but his group stayed put.

It remained a tense night, one that felt like it could explode at any moment.

I was wracked with uncertainty, but I prayed deeply. I prayed for Zahra's safety, and for Ahtmar's. And I prayed we would survive the journey.

The next morning, I awoke to frightful screams, and the sounds of blades clashing. I scrambled to my feet and searched for the signs of battle. In the middle of camp, near the extinguished fire, Ahtmar had locked swords with Aazim. Their group of Seljuks surrounded them. Zahra was behind them with her hands clasped.

I just about tumbled down the hill as I raced to the camp. Ahtmar punched Aazim in the jaw, and the larger man crashed to the dirt. He rolled to his feet and swung wildly at Ahtmar, who evaded and slashed his target's hand. Now that I was close, I saw the blood spurt from the wound as Aazim lost the grip on his sword. Ahtmar held his weapon to Aazim's throat as the large man kneeled, defeated.

"What have you got to say now?" Ahtmar asked as he stared down at him. Suddenly, he laughed. It was pained. "You even scored the first blow." I hadn't noticed at first, but once he said it, my eyes were drawn to a cut in his side, cleaved through his armor, ripped through fabric. The deep red color bled through.

"I'm at your mercy," Aazim replied. His head dropped, which left Ahtmar's sword at the top of his neck instead.

Ahtmar breathed in, held it in his chest, and then exhaled deeply. "Those of you who agree with Aazim… step forward."

The three others who threatened me last night obeyed the order.

Ahtmar eyed them, one at a time, until he settled on one man.

"Omar, right?" he asked. The man nodded. "Kneel."

"I won't." The rebel tensed up and brought his weapon up in front of him.

Ahtmar glanced at Aazim. "You're strong, and you're a good soldier. I still believe you to be useful. So you watch this – you absorb this – and you realize who leads you." His last words seemed to echo.

In a flash, Ahtmar knocked Omar's weapon away. He stabbed the man in the gut. The screams he let loose chilled me. His strength left him with each second. I watched in horror as the bloody, lifeless body crumpled to the earth.

"You will never be forgiven if you threaten my sister," Ahtmar continued. He knelt in front of Aazim and snatched a bunch of his clothes by his neck. His next words were fiery and ferocious: "I will defend my home, and my brothers – that includes you. But I will go to any length in this world to protect Zahra. Do you understand me?" The larger man nodded quickly, and hardly blinked.

"And Aazim," Ahtmar said as he let go of his firm grasp, "think about who the real enemy is. I am giving you another chance at life…" He pointed out to the distance, to the path we would soon follow. "While those men in silver slaughter our brothers. Think, Aazim." He focused on the eldest of his group. Suddenly, Ahtmar seemed sad. His burning energy dimmed. "Hilal… please… if you would?"

Hilal stepped forward. "Ahtmar is right," he said. "Were I leading you, as I did many moons ago, I would say the same thing: we must stand together against the greatest threat in our history."

Aazim, to my surprise, rose with no hostility. He bowed his head and pressed a fist into his chest. Then, he walked away. His two remaining conspirators trailed after him. Ahtmar pulled Zahra away into his tent I was left utterly speechless.

Ahtmar had been brutal, but as I considered what we'd done to the Turks… I wondered if I would've been any different in his position. More than that – he had done it to protect his family.

Eventually, the chaotic emotions settled in camp, and we got back on the road. I galloped alongside the group but kept my distance. I glanced at Zahra often as she rode behind her brother. She was paler than usual. I wanted to talk to her, even comfort her, but I knew it wasn't my place. I had to keep focused on the future.

For the next handful of days, I found fleeting moments to say hello to her, but didn't manage more. The rest of the time, I was heat-stricken and surrounded by a group who suspiciously eyed each other. I was filled with unease, and my whole body felt tight and heavy. Somehow, we made it through the trek with no further violence. We arrived at our destination the following morning: the fortress of Antioch.

We stopped on a ridge and overlooked the fortress. Stone towers and walls as far as the eye could see. Turks patrolled and manned the defenses in numbers I couldn't count. I thought of Adhemar, and how he had described Antioch as the knights' greatest hurdle. Despite the fact that he left me behind, part of me hoped he was all right.

I hadn't exchanged a word with Ahtmar for several days, but he suddenly rode up to me. Zahra peeked out from behind him and faintly smiled at me.

"Julien," Ahtmar began, "I want you to wait here. I'm going to…" He paused, and it was strange. It was like he lost track of his thoughts. "You stay here. All right?"

"Sure," I replied with a bow of my head.

He shifted his horse towards his group. "Hilal? Over here."

The elder man approached and eagerly awaited Ahtmar's words.

"You remain here with Julien. I am going to tell our brothers at Antioch about him. I can't guarantee they won't become hostile when I do, so I'm putting Zahra in your care. Do you understand? I don't do this lightly."

"I understand," Hilal said. "I will protect her with my life." He frowned. "You're going to ask if we can enter the city – to defend it?"

Then, I felt many eyes on me.

The thought ran through my head quickly and swirled darkly. Defending a Turkish fortress... from my own allies? No...

Ahtmar's eyes lingered on me. Zahra hopped off his horse and jumped on Hilal's. Ahtmar then returned to the rest of his group. "My brothers!" he shouted as he brought a fist in the air. "With me! It's time to prepare for our last battle!"

They raced towards the towering front gates of Antioch and left the three of us by ourselves.

"Julien," Hilal said, "what we just asked of you is no small thing. Set that aside for a moment. How are you feeling?"

I blinked quickly. "I'm... I honestly don't know." I ran a hand across my horse's back. She breathed heavily in the heat.

"This all must be hard for you. But I appreciate that you've been honest and respectful with us. You even took the time to learn our language – not many would have."

I half-smiled. "Thanks. I will say, though, it hasn't been all bad for me." I thought about Zahra, but I didn't look at her. "And I might say I'm hopeful that I can talk to my leaders. Maybe we could avoid this. All of this."

"They could also simply cut you down."

"Hilal!" Zahra said. "He's trying to help us."

154

"It's okay," I replied. "We'll have to see what happens, won't we?"

"Indeed." Hilal nodded. "Now that you mention it, maybe we should see what Ahtmar is doing?"

I looked out at his group. They had made it to the gates, and they were communicating with someone atop the walls. "I'm definitely wondering if they've mentioned me."

"Well, I am too. Let's investigate."

"Are you sure, Hilal?" Zahra asked. "My brother won't be happy if he sees us."

"There's some cover down there in the trees. We'll be careful."

"I didn't know you were so adventurous." She mustered a small laugh.

"You weren't even born when I was adventuring, young lady." He grinned, but it quickly faded. "But I want to see if we can work together to stop this war."

"I'm willing to join you," I said.

"Then let's go."

We raced down the ridge into the trees, hopefully disguised to avoid being spotted, and then we hopped down off our horses. The three of us snuck close enough to hear the conversation at the gates.

"Let me speak to your leader, please," Ahtmar pleaded.

"All right," came a quick reply from a guard on the wall. "But I doubt anyone would accept the offer you've just made."

After about a minute, another man came into view near the guard. He towered over the other soldier. He had a long, full beard, and a big smile peeked through as he saw Ahtmar.

"Ahtmar Naji," he boomed. "I'm glad you survived, my boy."

"Elchanes?" Ahtmar replied. His voice peaked in excitement. "I'm happy you made it, too. Are you in charge of Antioch?"

"At the request of Kilij Arslan, yes." The man sighed deeply. "The knights have been chasing me halfway across Anatolia."

"They're coming here next. They must be."

"I know." Elchanes ran a hand through his beard. "So what's this I hear – you've captured one of them?"

"Not exactly. He defected."

"I find that hard to believe."

"It's true," Naasir shouted. "He even speaks our language – crudely. But he seems genuine."

"I'm not sure if I agree," Aazim loudly grumbled. He might've been right. Truly, I hadn't been certain where I stood.

"There is discontent among you, clearly," Elchanes maintained. "The fact that you haven't brought him before me tells me a great deal." He held his arms out to the side. "So how is it that I can allow him in here, when you don't even know his allegiance?"

"I will take responsibility for him," Ahtmar said.

The towering Turk nodded slowly. "You've always been true to your word." He paused. "But I want to meet him."

Ahtmar hesitated. "All right, sir."

The brotherhood turned their horses, ready to summon us from the hill. Rather than remain hidden, we mounted our horses, and Hilal called out to announce us.

His words, and my sudden presence, got an understandable response. Dozens of bows were aimed at us from the walls. I followed Hilal as he moved up. I kept my hands in the air.

"What are you doing?" Ahtmar barked at us. "I told you to stay back."

"I'm sorry, my friend," Hilal said meekly. "But we are all part of this battle. That might even include Julien."

The young Turk shook his head. Elchanes said, "There is no

control among your group, Ahtmar. You disappoint me." He flicked his head towards the elder. "And you, too, Hilal."

Ahtmar said, "Julien's presence here has thrown things out of alignment. But… I believe his arrival here is part of a divine plan."

"Do you, now? And what does the boy in silver and crimson have to say about that?" The bows remained trained on me as Elchanes studied me. "Well? Do you truly understand us?"

"I do," I said in Arabic. I took a long, full, anxious breath.

I'd found myself with an audience of Turks, most of whom were ready to be rid of me. As Hilal drifted towards Ahtmar with Zahra behind him, I was separated – alone.

Despite that, I couldn't disguise my feelings in order to survive. If I was to face God's judgment one day, I had to be honest, even to my supposed enemies.

The Turks waited patiently for my response, but Elchanes tapped his fingers on his folded arms. That was when it hit me – his name.

I recalled that it was my first mission – to find and kill him – and we had never discovered him. Could this be the same dreadful man that had massacred Peter's forces?

As if I couldn't have been any more uncertain about my place, I found myself paralyzed.

It was only when I looked at Zahra that I was able to break free. Her face was marked with sadness, but her eyes shone with hope.

I looked up at Elchanes, and the hot sun nearly blinded me. I lowered my hands and said, "Is it true that you killed an army of peasants?"

The man asked his guards to lower their weapons.

"Do you know what those peasants did when they arrived in Anatolia, young Julien? They massacred the first people that they

157

encountered: Christians." He paced as my heart raced. "They didn't even stop to ask who they were – they simply murdered them. Elderly people. Children – babies. They roasted children on spits."

My whole body felt heavy, and I felt sick. Deep down, buried in the furthest depths of my soul, I knew he had told me the truth.

"We were not happy about that. And do you know why? Because we care for Christians, too." Elchanes pointed behind him. "Indeed, there are some living here." He slowly nodded. "The people that inflicted such horror eventually came to find us. They slaughtered everyone at one of our garrisons."

I felt like I would pass out at any moment. I wavered on my horse. The terrible thoughts ran through my mind. That people from my home did such nightmarish things to others. That maybe even my father had.

"So what were we to do, Julien?" Elchanes pleaded. He peered out towards the horizon. "What are we to do, against an army that carries a religious fury that will burn everything in its path?"

"We can only defend ourselves," Ahtmar sadly said. "And try to stop the storm."

I couldn't help but cry. The truth washed over me, so cold and bitter, even under the blazing sun.

"Don't you see?" Ahtmar said to me. "You are meant to be here – alongside us."

I looked at him with tears in my eyes. He appeared distorted with my watery vision. I searched my soul, clawed into it with my mind, but I found no answer. Eventually, I settled on the only truth I found at the time. "Ahtmar... no matter what you've said, I can see nothing divine about my journey here." I quickly glanced at Zahra and felt a nauseating twinge in my heart. I faced her brother. "All I've seen... is hell."

I shook my head as I wept like a child. "I can't fight for you – I can't be with you. I can only wait for God to show me where I need to be."

The stunned Turks looked back at me, some angry, and some disappointed – Ahtmar perhaps most of all. Elchanes, though, might have been impressed.

"I appreciate your honesty," he said. "So I will be honest with you too: we can't accept you, Julien. You will have to leave."

The brotherhood watched me for what felt like a long time. They might've waited for me to change my mind, but I couldn't.

Then, the Turks opened the massive gates of Antioch. The brotherhood trotted inside, and the siblings' eyes lingered on me. The gates closed behind them.

The weight of loneliness pressed down on my shoulders. I wondered if this was what God wanted of me – to be alone.

I thought about going to Jerusalem. I still had my map, and a clear path to the holy land. But that was no answer. The notion made a pit in my stomach.

I had nothing left except for one mission: to face down my army – the people who I had once called friends – and ask them to stop this war.

I had made that promise to Zahra.

Chapter 14
A week later, one mile from Antioch

I stood in the center of the well-trod road to Antioch. I was wracked with nervousness, boiling hot from a blistering sun and chillingly cold from worry. How in the world was I going to convince Raymond to turn his army away? Would they just stampede over me, or cut me down?

My stomach grumbled, which pulled me from my thoughts. I'd survived on my own supplies, and now they had run low. As I'd discovered, I wasn't a great scout on my own, and an even worse forager. But I managed, and really, the worst part of this past week had been sleeping alone.

I dreamt often of Zahra – at least I had that.

Despite my inexperience scouting, in the morning I had seen a glimpse of the mighty Catholic army on its approach to Antioch. They were impossible to miss.

Soon, the ground rumbled beneath my feet, like a storm inside the earth itself.

I was downhill, so I would be able to see the army as it came over it. For excruciating minutes, I waited for Raymond.

As much as my promise to Zahra had meant, there was more to this reunion. I had my own questions to ask my former mentors. Why had they left me for dead? Was I too weak? Too kind? Was I unworthy in their eyes?

It might've been some type of heat sickness that caused it, but my nervousness shifted into anger. I was dressed in the same armor that the knights gifted to me – but my view was different than when I first put it on.

I said one last prayer as the storm of noise overwhelmed me: Lord, please give me the strength to see this through.

And then, they came into view. First, it was the leaders in their glowing armor – Raymond and Adhemar led the way. Bohemond, Tancred, and Godfrey were all there too. The numbers that followed them grew – soldiers, priests, and women – while the distance between us shrunk.

Something was strange about it, though. The first thing I noticed was there were very few horses. I kept an eye to the far horizon, and the trail of warriors was not as long as I anticipated. I saw the end of it, for one. I might have misremembered the size of our forces in the time we'd been apart, but I was still shocked. Did the Turks smash us in half?

I saw the pale, tired faces of the faithful. Shortly thereafter, Raymond noticed me. He too was without a horse, but he raced up to me.

"Julien?" he cried as he breathed heavy. "Is that you, boy?" He looked different. He was thin, almost sickly.

"It's me, Raymond," I said shakily.

He grabbed my arms, and I tensed up. "You're not a ghost," he said. "How did you survive...?"

I shook free of his grasp. "The Turks gave me a second chance."

He laughed. "Well, maybe you are some kind of apparition, if you're saying things like that."

The other leaders joined us, and Adhemar stood behind them. He didn't look at me.

"It's the truth," I said. "I'm here because the Turks allowed it. There was a small group, especially, and…" My words faded as I thought of Zahra. "Sir Raymond… why did you leave me behind?"

My mentor frowned. "Everything I said back there was the truth of it. I do not lie, Julien."

My lips quivered, and I squeezed my hands into fists. "That's it?"

"That's it." He nodded.

"And what now?" I growled.

"Well now – now you're here. Now you're alive. You survived." He showed a prideful smile, as if he was the one who saved my life.

"I have a request, sir."

"Do you?" Raymond rubbed his stubbly, unkempt gray beard. "Make it quick – we have business behind you."

"It's about Antioch. I want your army to turn away from this slaughter. There's been enough of it."

Raymond burst out laughing. It quickly spread to the soldiers behind them. The mockery swelled into exasperated, uproarious laughter. Adhemar was the only one who refrained.

I quickly realized how foolish the notion was. I had attempted to turn aside a tidal wave.

"Julien," Raymond said through more laughter, "do you have any idea what we've been through?" In a flash, his amusement faded. "You wouldn't, because you were captured. You should know what happened – I'll grant you that much." He raised a finger towards the clouds. "We climbed a mountain in this heat, we – we almost starved. And it rained, it poured like the tears of heaven. We lost

163

so many lives, horses, equipment – so much – through the heat, the water and mud. You can see, can't you? See what we've lost?"

I felt a twinge of sadness in my heart, but I pressed my mentor. "So there's no stopping you – no matter what?"

"There is only one end to this journey, Julien." He grabbed my shoulders. He remembered my injury, as he squeezed that side tighter. "That is with a mountain of dead unbelievers in our wake. A mountain bigger than the one we've had to climb, so large that it casts a crimson shadow over Jerusalem."

I took Raymond's arms into my grasp and pried them off of me. My mentor suddenly seemed impressed. I glared at him. I tried to see beyond his pictures of violence, to the man who had done so much for me. For a moment, I thought I saw it. A precious fragment of it.

He said, "What's that look for, Julien? Have you grown a spine? Or are you doing the bidding of these Turks?"

"No, they..." My heart wavered. "They didn't want me. They turned away my help."

"And so you see the truth of it. You might have sympathy for them, but they don't want it. They don't want you." He pressed a gauntleted finger into my chest.

I glanced at Adhemar, who finally met my eyes. He quietly said, "That is the truth."

As I stood there, I was confronted again with the loneliness that had haunted me. Even with thousands of people on my horizon, I felt like the only soul in Anatolia. But then, Raymond touched my arm softly.

"You survived, Julien," he softly said. He knelt down, and struggled somewhat as he did. "I think that is quite amazing, actually." Slowly, I began to feel like a boy again – like I'd rediscovered something I'd lost. Raymond turned his gaze to the rolling clouds. "This – this moment here – it may very well be divine intervention."

"How's that?" Tancred said with an odd grin. "You mean meeting this whelp again?"

Raymond slowly nodded, but it didn't seem like he'd heard Tancred. He said, "You are my student – my protégé. I forged you into the man you are, but I made mistakes. I didn't... I didn't give you a chance to truly learn what was expected of you." He tapped my arm softly. "I was the cause of your failure."

"Sir...?" I barely managed. Raymond had disarmed me. I felt weaker and weaker as I gave in to my foolish past.

Raymond raised a silver finger in front of me. "One more, Julien." He paused grimly. "One more chance. What do you say?"

"I disagree with this," Bohemond grumbled. "I say we toss the boy's body into a ditch. He's a liability."

"Silence," Raymond suddenly shouted as he shot to his feet. "We've lost enough, haven't we?" He turned to his closest men, and the leaders of this army. "Haven't we?" he boomed.

"Yes, sir," came a collective, mighty roar from the soldiers. The Italians, and Godfrey, eyed me in hostility, but Adhemar smiled.

Raymond turned back to me. "What do you say, my boy? Join us and reclaim your place by my side. Let us both do God's will."

I raised my shoulders with a big, emotional sigh, and I found a smile of my own – the most regretful in my life. "Yes, Sir Raymond!"

"That's my boy." He grinned and gave me a big hug. Then, he approached my horse. "Ahh, there she is. Did you name her yet?"

"No, sir, I hadn't... I hadn't thought of one yet."

"Well, maybe she'll respond better to me, then. My legs are tired, you see. I'm an old man, and we've had quite a journey." He offered a boisterous, but distressing laugh. He took my horse from me.

The army resumed its march, and they picked up speed quickly, as if they'd found a new charge of energy. I scrambled to keep up, and I warned Raymond, "There's something else, sir. Elchanes is at Antioch. He's the general we've been after."

"Wonderful," he replied. "All the more reason you were led back to us. You'll help us avenge our fellow Frenchmen." He patted my head like I was a pet.

Slowly, without realizing it, I fell behind the army. I stared at the dusty ground. My inner emotions spun in turmoil. I sprinted to catch up with Raymond, who had hardly noticed I was gone.

Adhemar, though, walked up beside me. "Each night," he began, "I prayed for you, Julien. Each night, I wished for your safe return."

"Thank you, sir…" I avoided his gaze at first. "But you left me behind, too. Why..?"

The blonde-haired knight looked to the sky. "Sometimes, we have to trust the Lord above all else." He met my eyes intently. "That day, God took you from us, and delivered you into the enemy's hands. Raymond said it cruelly, but it was true – we allowed God to attend to your fate." He paused with a slight but hopeful smile. "But here you are, Julien. God works in ways we can never understand. Despite appearances, this is meant to be." The bishop smiled full and true, and wrapped his arm around me.

I didn't feel any warmth. I only felt pure chaos in my heart.

"Julien." Adhemar suddenly spoke with intensity, which summoned my attention.

"Yes, sir?"

"You need to figure out where you stand. As I look at you now… I don't see the fire of passion that burned when I first met you. What is it that you want, Julien?"

"I… I'm not sure. It's more complicated than I expected." I drifted away from the bishop. "I've gotten to know some of the Turks – they're not all bad."

"Is this journey not a holy duty?" He narrowed his eyes.

"I don't know. I just don't know anymore. It doesn't feel like it."

"Despite my doubts, I believe it is. I have a purpose – you must find yours. God brought you here for a reason."

"My purpose…?"

"After that, I might revisit the holy city. It may offer a new purpose. Why don't you go, too?"

I raised my head. "That's what I was planning."

"Then when the battle is done, we'll meet there, Julien. In the meantime – stay safe." He bowed his head and left.

It was like my nightmares. I was seeing my friends leave me behind again as I watched them walk away.

I'd gotten no answers, no clarity from this – and worse, I couldn't deter them from their path of war.

I rejoined my army as we continued our march towards the fortress of Antioch.

––––––––––

By the next day, the Catholic army had surrounded Antioch – or as much as it could, considering the miles-long walls. Our forces had already started work on siege weapons. In this case, we had built perriers. Unlike the rams that had battered Nicaea, the perriers were stationary, capable of hurling huge rocks over the walls of the city from a distance.

Raymond said it was because the city was too well-defended to use rams, and because the Turks would burn the wood if the rams got close. As I observed the city walls, I saw the glint of fiery braziers prepared to do just that.

But unlike my mentor, I wasn't focused purely on the battle. Secretly, I scanned the walls for the brotherhood – and for Zahra. I wondered how I could get her out of this disaster – and how I could save this city from a massacre. But I had no idea. I was the boy in-between.

Every so often, I thought I saw Zahra on the wall, with her dress waving lightly in the wind. But they were just shadows. They had to be. She would never want to see me again.

As the energy of war thrummed, my hope for the future waned.

Chapter 15

The sunny day was masked behind a gray, overcast sky, and the rain fell.

I watched the battlefield from a hill, with Raymond by my side. The forces below us stirred. Weapons were drawn. Bows were strung and arrows were counted. Excited voices echoed. The energy swirled and picked up. The feeling of battle swelled. The towers and walls of Antioch were fully manned. It was an endless stream of soldiers who looked to defend this fortress city.

I couldn't blame them for wanting to protect this place, even if my allies did. As Elchanes had said, there were Christians inside, along with Turks. I'd mentioned that to Raymond the night before, and all I had received in response was a scoff.

But no matter what, I couldn't run. Returning home to France was an impossibility. Fleeing to the holy land – and leaving my friends behind – was an even darker image.

All that remained was to leap into the fires of war once more. To see if, somehow, God might reveal His guidance if I persevered just a little longer.

I couldn't kill in cold blood. I knew that much. I couldn't

butcher any Turks, Christians, or anyone, as my knightly allies so desperately wanted to. But I had to fight – for an answer.

I had no more time to think. A stray arrow was fired from Antioch. It whistled through the air and crashed into the throat of a knight. My iron-clad allies called out a battle cry and raced towards the walls. Arrows rained down from the towers of Antioch, and in response, we sent our own volleys back.

Soldiers manned the siege weapons. They placed heavy rocks in the nets and pulled down on a huge rope to let them loose. The rocks hurled through the air and smashed into men on the walls. Their screams pierced through me. When more boulders flew, some warriors on the towers fled back into the city.

Raymond demanded the army bury the wall in arrows, which didn't work. We quickly learned just how defensible Antioch was.

I sprinted into the battlefield, deflected arrows coming towards me. I shielded my allies as best I could. Most of them didn't want my help. They shouted for me to leave.

I returned to Raymond's side and watched him direct the battle. Anytime a Turk fell from the wall, wounded, the knights pounced and stabbed and hacked off limbs. I couldn't look.

Eventually, we pulled back and reassessed our strategy. It was decided by the leaders that the siege would persist as long as possible, and then, we would starve out the city. Mere hours of battle seemed to have lasted for days.

The notion of being here any longer sunk my spirit, but this was just the beginning.

The next morning, the siege on Antioch remained at a standstill. We waited for some kind of opportunity to arise. It didn't happen that day, or the next.

The cries of war woke me up early the following morning.

Turks raced out from the city gates. There were hundreds of them on horseback, and they blasted arrows across the battlefield. I grabbed my shield and scrambled to my feet.

Once again, I took to Raymond's side, but as I stood right beside him, I'd never felt more distant from my mentor. Still, I held my shield up to protect him. I watched our archers cut down a line of the Turks' horses and tried in vain to block out the violence. I'd never learned how to use a bow. I might've been more useful if I had – but I had no interest in learning another way to kill.

I stood at the front of the group to protect whoever I could. That's all I felt I could do.

When the battle relented, the fields outside of Antioch were littered with bodies – but they were mostly Turks. The survivors retreated inside the gates of Antioch, which slammed shut with a booming crash. Our forces had been too far away to chase them inside.

Raymond, infuriated, sent his men over to the recently slain Turks. Bohemond and Tancred joined in the effort and sent their own troops to individual corpses. The knights chopped off the Turks' heads.

I was nauseated. My spirit felt so low that it threatened to pull me into the earth.

That day, the siege weapons – the perriers – heaved the bloody, severed heads of the Turks into Antioch.

I had a vision of Ahtmar, I think, somewhere in the haze of my memories. I had seen him so distraught, so unnerved and pale, as he stood on one of the walls. I still don't know if it was real, but… how could it not have been?

And Zahra – I couldn't bear to think what she had gone through.

Despite the horror of seeing their allies' heads thrown back at them, Antioch's Turks didn't surrender. The siege persisted for days, which turned into weeks. There was nowhere to go, nothing to do but wait for the answer I so desperately needed.

I had no one to lean on. Raymond spent his time on battle plans and hardly acknowledged me. Somewhere along the way, Adhemar had gotten sick. He slept often. None of the other leaders even looked me in the eye – I was a traitor to them.

The temperatures fell, and I barely endured. The rains persisted. On one stormy morning, I finally received what I needed – an answer.

It was another sudden burst of battle under the morning sun. The Turks roared out of the gates in droves, covered by a hail of arrows from the walls and towers. Things had been at a standstill for so long by that point that it felt like an ambush.

Raymond was able to organize the men. He formed sections of defenses and sent out waves of his own cavalry to chase the nimble Turks.

I was left stunned. The brotherhood was among the group of attackers. At the forefront was Ahtmar, and even more shockingly, Zahra squeezed him for dear life. Why is she here? I frantically wondered. Why would be bring her into the battle?

I knew Ahtmar must've had a reason. While the knights did battle with the Turks, I was off in my own world as I watched the frenzied assault of the small group of Turks. Hilal and Nassir fought confidently and sent multiple knights to the ground with swift strikes. Even the younger ones, Bekir and Sami, fought valiantly to defend Antioch – and Ahtmar.

The wind roared, and thunder cracked through the sky as rain poured on this awful battle.

I suddenly felt called to move.

While Raymond wasn't looking, I took my horse back. My

172

mentor had been too distracted to notice. I chased after Ahtmar as his group trekked along the miles-long stone fortress. Along the way, several members of the brotherhood were caught by arrows or stray melee attacks from the knights. They toppled off of their horses. The young Sami remained alive until the knights caught up and killed him.

Ahtmar had seen it happen, and his expression was frozen grief.

Eventually, the brotherhood escaped the massive reach of the silver army. They stopped on a hill overlooking the battle, and I was not far behind. I pulled up short, using the trees as cover.

Ahtmar sat quietly, and Zahra held onto him tightly. She pulled him back towards her as she cried. The brother stared at the battle, at the way his allies were once again being swarmed and routed by the merciless knights, and his eyes turned cold. He wore a long, hopeless face, and eventually his head dropped.

My heart pounded. I was torn between my past – the knights, and everything I had learned – and the Turks, who had saved me, and showed me that there was so much more to learn. I needed to decide where to go – where I belonged.

With Raymond, all I had found was death and destruction. With the Turks, I had found hope and understanding. This moment hadn't been what I'd truly wanted – a light from heaven to pierce the clouds and shine upon where I should've gone – but God had granted me the time I needed to make perhaps my most important decision.

I moved toward the Turks.

As I did, I noticed Aazim and two others moving toward Ahtmar. Their killing intent was clear, as it had been when they had turned it on me.

"Ahtmar!" I called, and he looked at me, utterly shocked. "Look out!"

There was no time for him to defend himself, but I knew it was my time to save him like he had me. As I raced ahead, I jumped off of my horse and right into Aazim. I tackled him from his steed. The big man let out an airless gasp as we crashed to the hard ground.

The other two conspirators wheeled away, and in that time, Ahtmar collected himself. He ordered Hilal and Naasir to chase them while I struggled for control with Aazim. He was much stronger than me. He fought me away with a heavy punch, but I responded with one of my own.

Hilal killed one of our foes, and Naasir felled the other with a precise arrow. Ahtmar hopped down from his horse and marched up to us with a fire in his eyes. Under the dark sky, in the pouring rain, it was scary.

A heartbeat later, Hilal joined me, and helped me hold Aazim down.

"Why have you done this?" Ahtmar shouted. He hadn't spoken to me. In a strange way, it was already like I was part of the brotherhood – his trustworthy ally. The Turk swung his sword wildly, angrily. "You would turn on us now, Aazim?"

"I should lead us, not you!" the man raged. He tried to hit me, and I narrowly evaded it. Hilal grabbed one arm while I held the other. "You're a useless fool who will get us all killed with your indecision! We should have stayed and fought to the bitter end!"

"I'm through with battle!" Ahtmar cried. "I wanted us to leave – to finally go to Jerusalem and ask God for guidance. If we stay, we will all be killed."

"You dishonor the Turks. You're a coward."

"No," the boy said, much more softly. "I simply see when all is lost." He paused with an emotional sigh. "And I will not allow Zahra to die. I told you before – I will do anything on this earth to preserve her life."

Aazim struggled harder to get free. "Let me go! If you're not a coward, then fight! Fight me to see who should lead!"

Ahtmar's face turned dark, blotted out by a pitch-black shadow. It didn't suit him, but the world had cast its darkness on him.

He knelt and pressed his kilij firmly into Aazim's neck. "There may have been a time when you deserved a fight," he grimly said. "But when you threatened my sister, you forfeited that. When you sought to attack me from behind – and cleave through her to get to me – no, you don't have the right any longer." He inhaled deeply and exclaimed, "Zahra! Look away!"

The girl let loose a cry of terror, but she listened. I was frozen, but my instincts tricked me. I kept Aazim trapped. Ahtmar stood and pressed his boot down on his blade. The cries of Aazim were worthy only of nightmares. I looked away, but the sounds of flesh and bone being severed were almost worse than the image of the bloody deed.

When Aazim fell silent, I rolled off of him, horrified. I barely held back my sickness.

Hilal was equally affected. He quickly retreated from the body.

When I looked back at Ahtmar, he stood tall and held his bloody sword high in the air. The brotherhood pressed their fists into their chests in solidarity. Ahtmar's display was one of a leader – it was to give the illusion that everything was all right, so that a glimmer of hope might remain.

Zahra had her hands over her face. As they slid down, the rain ran down her face, but I knew it was mixed with tears. "No," she said as she sobbed. "This... horror, this violence... this isn't you, brother."

The boy turned to meet her, and there seemed to be a great distance between them, even if they were within inches of one

175

another. He hugged his sister and said, "I know. But I've told you countless times – no one will hurt you. No one will take you from me – from this world. You're all I have…" Ahtmar struggled not to break down. His body shook. But as he held his sister, as they swayed in the rain, he seemed to become calm.

Strangely, the battle behind us had quieted down around the same time. Raymond and the knights had pulled back once again.

I trembled. Now that Aazim and his allies were dead, the brotherhood turned to face me.

"You came back," Ahtmar quietly said.

I grabbed a fistful of the earth and slammed my other into the ground. "This is wrong. All of it." My own tears fell and mixed with the wet soil.

"Julien," I heard Zahra whisper. "You saved me. You saved us."

I raised my head. "No, I… I rejoined the French army, I…"

"Stay with us, for now," Hilal said, with a lightness that lifted my spirits. The elder Turk showed the slightest of smiles, and he reached out a hand for me. The Turk helped me out of the dirt.

———————

The stormy day faded into a humid night. We made camp away from the battle, out of sight, and went without a fire to disguise our presence. In the darkness, I sat across from the brotherhood, as most of them couldn't sleep. Hilal had taken guard duty, and he observed the silent battlefield every few minutes in case we were being hunted. As far as we knew, all of us had escaped the attention of the knights, and I truly didn't expect Raymond cared that I was gone.

I held my knees into my chest and watched Ahtmar hold Zahra close. She had fallen asleep, and I saw a glint of her tears under the faint starlight. Her brother brushed them away with his thumb.

I stood and stepped away. I had to clear my mind. I ended up between two tall trees. I looked up at the wet leaves that waved in the wind and tried to see beyond the sky to the heavens. A branch cracked behind me. I barely contained my fright as I took a defensive battle stance with my sword at the ready.

It was Ahtmar and Zahra. The brother quickly drew his sword – probably a reaction to what I did. Slowly, we both relaxed.

"I wanted to thank you," Ahtmar said.

"Oh. Of course…"

"You saved my sister's life. And you saved mine too. Aazim would've had no problem killing us both."

I avoided the boy's gaze. "Yes, I…I may be uncertain on almost everything right now, but I know I didn't want that to happen."

"What about me, Julien? Do you trust me?"

"I don't know." I glanced at Zahra. "But your sister shouldn't have to go through this. She's kind, and good. She's…" I looked at Ahtmar.

The boy stared at me, and for the first time in a long while, I felt hostility from him, masked among the shadows of the night. He firmly said, "I know."

I held my hands up in defense. "I would never hurt her. You must be able to tell that about me."

Ahtmar tensed a fist. "Just remember what I said earlier – do you understand?" Zahra tugged on his arm, and shook her head. "What?" her brother asked. She didn't answer.

To that point, the obvious danger of having feelings for Zahra hadn't even occurred to me. Eventually I said, "I understand."

Ahtmar glared at me before he returned to camp. I spent the night out among the trees.

Chapter 16

For the next several days, we waited. We watched the battles, the standstills, and the failed sieges of the knights. We watched the Turks rally in defense, and Antioch remained unbroken.

We all wanted to leave. We wanted to go to Jerusalem. The path was clear – we didn't have to stay and struggle.

For Ahtmar and the brotherhood, they couldn't stand to leave their allies behind. They planned a counterattack for days. But what good was a small group of warriors, no matter how skilled, against thousands of knights?

I couldn't leave either. For my Turkish allies, but also for me. If the knights broke through the gates of Antioch, it would be a massacre unlike any other. I thought of going back to Raymond, but I knew he couldn't be stopped, unless by force. And that wasn't something I could do.

There was a positive part of this long wait – Zahra had tried to teach Ahtmar Latin. I overheard them once. Apparently, the girl had secretly learned the language while her brother had trained to fight back against us.

Many nights, I heard the two practice Latin words. For a while, her brother was reluctant – much like I was when I first learned Arabic – but I appreciated his effort.

We may have had different religions, but all of us waited for a sign from above, a guiding light that would shine down and reveal our collective path. For a long time, it didn't happen. All we could do was trust in God, no matter how difficult that could sometimes be.

One evening, while dusk coated nature in an orange glow, the shadows seemed darker than usual. Zahra and her brother had separated from the group as I often had, and they shared a hug. From where I sat, I overheard their conversation.

"Happy birthday, sister."

"Thanks. I'm glad we have a little time to enjoy it."

"It won't be much longer now. I can feel it."

"Yes. Well, Ahtmar – can we talk about me making my own decisions?"

"I did promise you I'd speak about this on your birthday. I'll tell you what – you can introduce me to the man you want to be with. I'll still judge him harshly, though, and it is still my decision to make."

"Ahtmar…"

"You're everything to me, sister. I want you to be with someone who can keep you safe, someone I can trust. I can't lose you."

"I know. I don't want to lose you, either."

Ahtmar sighed deeply. "You'll tell me when you find him, right?"

"I'd like to."

"Good. I suppose I'll have to prepare myself for when that day comes, years from now…"

I rested on my back and tried to sleep, but truly, all I thought about was who that man would be – the one who would be with Zahra.

When I woke, the moon was still high. I heard distant words, so

I turned over and looked back to where our camp was. Hilal was stalwart on guard duty. He watched Antioch with eagle eyes. But he hadn't been the one who spoke. I scanned the trees beyond the camp, and I saw Ahtmar and Zahra again.

This time, risky as it was, I approached them. They stood behind a large tree, so I kept low and quiet until I saw them from the side. Ahtmar held Zahra's hands tightly. I knelt and listened.

"Sister – do you still have the dagger I gave you, back in Nicaea?"

"I made a wrapping around my leg for it."

"Show me." Zahra glanced away. She was embarrassed. "Please." Her brother turned away as the girl lifted her dress. I gasped and looked away. My cheeks were completely flushed. I gave it a few moments, and then glanced back with one eye closed. Zahra held a dagger tightly.

"Good," Ahtmar concluded. "Just in case."

"Yes… just in case."

I looked away again as Zahra returned the dagger to its hiding place, and then quickly scurried back to my place in the camp. Ahtmar would, as he said, protect his sister no matter what.

———

Several days later, when our collective hope had run dry, a path through the chaos finally emerged. But it wasn't ours, yet – it was mine.

The skies were clear, and the moon was full. I sat on the hill near our darkened camp and watched the long stone walls that seemed to stretch forever. I noticed a small group of knights, about ten, as they rode along the walls. They stopped near one of the towers. I squinted. I saw faint candlelight from the tower's window.

Zahra and Ahtmar rested near me. "Hey," I said as I tapped the brother carefully on the side. I was tired. I spoke in Latin without

181

realizing it: "You should see this – there are some knights by the walls. I think I recognize them."

Ahtmar stirred and sat up. I pointed out to what I had seen. He perked up a little more. "What's going on?" he asked. "You recognize who?"

"You understood me, Ahtmar?"

He paused. "I think I got most of it."

I smiled in a way I hadn't done in a while. He looked at me like I was crazy. I couldn't blame him. But my smile soon dipped. "I should go to them. I should confront them."

"We could take the fight to them. They're a small group."

"No. We might alert the entire army." I sighed deeply. "Please – let me do this."

By now, the brotherhood had woken up. All of this brought a sudden burst of energy. It was the first sign of life, of change, in weeks. I took to my horse as Ahtmar studied me intently. I wondered if he trusted me – if he thought I might have simply returned to Raymond as an ally – but I pushed the notion to the back of my mind.

Zahra stirred too, and she looked up at me from her bedroll. "You're going, Julien?" she quietly asked.

"Yes." I sat up straight and gazed at the stars. "If there is a way for me to stop this assault on your people – I have to try." I looked at Zahra sadly. "I don't know if I'll make it back. The knights might just kill me."

She climbed to her feet and latched onto her brother. "If they attack," she pleaded, "we'll help him, right?"

Ahtmar glanced at his sister and narrowed his eyes, and then looked at me. Hilal said, "We'll help you, Julien. Isn't that right, Ahtmar?"

The leader hesitated. "Yes. We will shield you, if it comes to that." His words rung true to me.

"Stay safe, Julien," Zahra said with a soft smile. "And thank you."

I nodded and said goodbye to the brotherhood.

I skirted down the hill, towards the shadowy knights by the tower. One of the figures had been massive. I'd hoped it wasn't who I thought it was.

The knights drew their weapons upon my approach. I held my hands up and announced myself, and while that did prevent my death, it didn't make the men lower their swords. When I got closer, Bohemond's imposing presence became clear. He and Tancred walked a few steps towards me.

"It's you," Bohemond barked. "You're lucky we didn't kill you at first glance."

"What are you doing out here?" I asked.

"I've got nothing to say to you. You should get along to your master, if he still even wants you."

"I'm tired of being spoken to like this. I—"

I was cut off by a whistle from above – from the faintly lit tower. A voice followed: "Bohemond?"

"Aye," he firmly replied as he kept a steady, hostile glare on me. He finally relented, and looked up to the tower. "Are we clear?"

"We're clear." With that, whoever was in the tower dropped a long rope out the window.

Bohemond wore a smug smile as he faced me. "You want to know what we're doing, huh? We're winning this battle. Not everyone inside Antioch wants to keep us out. The faithful want to welcome us. I'll tell you what – if you want to help us, then you can come along. But don't blame me if your pathetic sympathy gets you killed."

"Fuck you!" I raged. I'd had enough of the knights' hostility –

and I was stir-crazy from waiting for so long. I let the anger go with an intentional breath. "Just give me a minute, please. I... have to prepare." I lied. I planned to warn Ahtmar.

"I'll give you nothing," Bohemond snapped. "Follow me or don't. I don't care." He patted Tancred on the shoulder. "Nephew, get back to Raymond. Let him know it's time to fight. I'll see you inside." The much younger knight bared his devilish grin and darted off into the moonlit fields.

Bohemond's group made their way up the rope. I was briefly frozen. There was no time to return to the Turks at camp and warn them. I had to go into the city to stop this disaster. I climbed down from my horse and petted her softly.

"I'm sorry," I whispered. "After all this time, I have no name for you. Do you still like me?" I forced an empty smile as she neighed. "Will you stay here for me, girl? Will you—" My words trailed off as I saw Ahtmar on the distant hill. "Okay, girl. Change of plans. Go!" I smacked her side, and she ran towards Ahtmar. I took a big, heavy breath, and waved goodbye to my Turkish ally. Then, I climbed the rope.

Inside the tower, there was an older man deep in prayer. He didn't seem to notice us. He whispered quietly to himself. I peeked back outside and saw the French army as it assembled in the darkness.

I exited through the only door in the tower and headed down a long flight of stairs, which circled around to the bottom. I crept out into the city of Antioch. I was only a few hundred feet from the front gates. Bohemond had just executed a guard. He pulled his massive, bloody sword out of the man's chest while the giant's nephew looked on, pleased. The rest of Bohemond's group crouched near the gate.

To my right, I had a good view of the city. There were many buildings, much like Nicaea, and they were dark. Most of the people inside must've been sleeping. There were businesses. I saw a forge and an empty marketplace. There was a church and a mosque which glimmered in the light from above. The rest of the buildings were homes – likely with civilians inside.

There were many guards on patrol, lit by the torches they carried. They hadn't been alerted yet. Bohemond looked at me and grabbed the huge piece of wood that kept the gates locked.

"Come here, Julien," he quietly barked.

I dashed next to him and knelt in cover.

"Prove yourself to me, boy. When we lift this gate, thousands will die. Prove to me that you're a man. A man who will kill for Christ. Then I will forgive you. Then I will accept you."

I stared at him coldly. My eyes drifted to his silver armor, which I'd been so foolishly infatuated with. Then to his unnerving grin, the expression of a man who was ready, and eager, to kill thousands in cold blood. And finally, to his allies, who were united in their bloodlust, their desire for personal power and victory. The torch light created shadows that danced across the faces and armor of these corrupt men.

At that moment, I understood what I was meant to do. I understood what I'd seen in my dreams – that shadowy army I had been so afraid of. And I was staring right at them.

Bohemond was sick of waiting. He snatched my hand and placed it on the wood next to his. "It's time, Julien. Stop looking at me like you hate me. You came here to do exactly what we're going to right now: end the lives of the unbelievers. Or are you a coward?"

I pulled my hand from his control, and I slowly shook my head. "No, Bohemond. I was a coward. But I was running from the truth."

185

"What the hell are you on about?" His allies shifted, and several of them pointed their blades in my direction.

"There is a cross to bear," I firmly said. "And there is a sword to wield." I pushed up to my feet, stepped back, and drew my sword. "But it's not against the Turks – it's against you."

Rather than be killed by the group of knights, I ran out into view of the Turkish guards. I yelled in Arabic, "Intruders! The Franks are inside Antioch! Take up your arms!" I grabbed a torch, waved it wildly, and tossed it in the direction of Bohemond.

The knights looked at me like I was a lunatic. And I smiled – full and true – as I charged towards them.

For the first time in my life, I was excited for battle. But not to kill, not to maim – rather, I served to distract the knights.

I fought one off, barely, and sent his sword aside with my own as he tried to lop off my head. I battered my shoulder into him, and he fell. My strength surprised me. Bohemond and another silver slayer tried to pull the wooden bar off the gate, but I smashed my sword into the smaller man, and then the monstrous Bohemond. The latter was barely affected by my attack, but he was enraged enough that he turned his giant blade on me.

By now, the Turks had assembled, and they swarmed towards the gates. My time to escape waned. As I narrowly avoided death at Bohemond's blade, a thought crept into my mind.

Is this it, dear God? Is this where you would have me offer my life to you? Do you wish to question me – have me answer for my sins? On the next swing, Bohemond slammed his sword into the ground, and cracked a vicious fist into my jaw. I crashed to the earth and stared up at the sky. My vision was a black blur.

God... I know deep inside that these men are wrong. They've

always been wrong. So why are they winning this war? Why won't you stop this?

The heavens were silent. There was only my blurred vision and desperate heart. I tilted my chin down. Bohemond had lifted his massive weapon above me, ready to end me in one swing. Behind him, his knights had grabbed hold of the wooden planks that separated the Turks from a nightmare army.

I saw shadows on the edges of my vision. The Turks of Antioch were not far.

I have more to give, God. I can stop this madness. If you would have me die here, to stop this massacre – I will. Please – tell me now. Tell me what I must do.

And then, the knights lifted the barrier. The gate was dragged open to reveal innumerable knights, who glittered under the stars. There was a frozen moment of fear as I knew it was over. That I'd failed, and then, the invaders let loose cries of pure passion and rage. It was a terrifying howl unlike anything I'd ever heard. The noise of monsters who had been deprived of their merciless violence for much too long.

As they charged ahead, towards me, they looked like silver demons who poured out of hell's gate.

Bohemond peered down at me and smiled. He swung down, but I rolled to the side and avoided the killing blow. I scrambled to my feet, which kicked up a storm of dust, and faced down the towering knight. But in only a heartbeat, I was swarmed by knights, who quickly splintered off and sprinted into the streets of Antioch in frenzy.

I don't know quite what happened. It might've been my armor, which could've identified me as an ally to their bloodlust-red vision, but the knights battered through me without killing me.

I suppose it could've been God who protected me, too. But I think, by then, I'd realized that it wasn't me who needed protection.

I endured the seemingly endless tide of knights, being stepped on hundreds of times in their charge, and I felt something in my body snap. I just breathed, and prayed, and held my hands over my head to preserve myself.

When the dust settled, it was briefly eerily quiet. I weakly pushed myself to my feet and saw Bohemond and Tancred across from me. They looked at me with cruel certainty.

"Now you'll see how you've failed, whelp," Tancred coldly said.

"Just watch, Julien," Bohemond said as he hoisted his blade over his shoulder. "Watch and weep." The two knights took off into the city.

The stream of silver demons spread out to the entire city like a disease. They paid little mind to the small amount of defenders who pelted them with arrows. The bulk of the Turks had only woken up.

Soon, the knights swarmed into the buildings. And then, the screaming started.

I breathlessly watched as the knights cut down guards by the dozens. Civilians fled their homes – they were cut down just the same in a fiery, malicious passion that left blood spattered in the streets and bodies toppled over one another.

I tried desperately to block out the sounds of violence – the swords on bone and flesh, the shrieks of terror from men and women – but it didn't work. My whole body was wound up tightly. I couldn't fight an entire army on my own, but I had missed my best chance to stop the massacre. The weight pressed down on my shoulders, and I fell to my knees.

Just as my tears fell to the earth, I felt a hand on my shoulder.

"Get up, Julien." It was Ahtmar, and he had brought my horse. I looked up at him, stunned. "Rise." The brotherhood was there – except for Hilal and Zahra. "If we're to die, then let's do it together."

I swallowed my sadness and shot to my feet. "Yes."

I readied my sword and shield, and Ahtmar finally told me, "Thank you for trying."

We raced after the knights. The brotherhood killed several in their initial arrow volley. Quickly, the rabid warriors were alerted to the threat, and they pushed towards us.

I caught one knight by surprise, who had thought I was an ally. It pained me, but I cut him down. I shielded Naasir from a stray mace blow and knocked another knight out with my sword hilt. Bekir finished that one for me.

Several of the brotherhood died in a return volley from the knights. Their bodies fell limp behind us.

I fought with more anger than I'd expected. Rather than the fires of zealous passion, I swung my blade in hatred – at the knights, at the circumstances, and with the belief I would soon be dead.

As I barely felled another former ally, he slammed his mace into my chest in his death throes. I hit the ground with no air in my lungs.

In my haze, I pondered if my death would be quick, and how soon after that I would face God's judgment. I looked up from the ground to see a knight standing over me, with murderous rage in his eyes and a sword held high, and that's when I truly felt my life had been claimed by God.

But somewhere in my mind, another thought took precedence. It hadn't been a voice I heard – more of a feeling that I translated into words. I had more to do. A vision of Jerusalem flashed before my eyes.

Should Antioch fall, which by then was a certainty, these monsters would push on and destroy the holy land. I knew they would show no mercy. I knew their hatred would burn at its searing peak in God's city. If I died now, I couldn't defend that holy place. I couldn't pray where the Lord's light shines the brightest.

As the knight's blade came down towards my head, I moved. And then I fought back.

I had to go to Jerusalem. I needed to speak with God there, to find my answers.

I knocked the knight's sword aside. I used all of my power and hope, and I ended the man's life with one final swing from my sword.

And I must save Zahra.

We were pushed back towards the gates as more and more of the knights gravitated to us. By that point, few of the Turkish defenders survived. Many of them had holed up inside a distant barracks, which the silver demons attempted to break into.

The bravest Turks, the ones who had resigned themselves to their deaths, showered arrows on the knights from the walls as they were chased down.

But that was just it. I couldn't resign myself. Not yet. If there came a time, I was prepared to make that sacrifice, but only when I knew it was time. As I looked at the brotherhood, they looked back, almost in unison. It was as though we had all realized the same thing. Ahtmar and I nodded at one another.

The Turk leader ordered the brotherhood to retreat, while he and I covered their escape.

In a moment I will remember forever, Ahtmar and I stood back-to-back, impossible allies united. We pointed our swords at a common enemy – an army of thousands of knights.

A large section was charging towards us.

"You will never hurt my friend," I desperately screamed. Ahtmar looked at me.

"Friend...?" he quietly said. Then, somehow, he managed to laugh. "Friend." He rallied and thrust a fist into the air.

While Ahtmar fired his bow towards the ocean of warriors, I hopped on my horse. I shielded him from a round of arrows.

Then, we retreated. We blasted out of the gates and into the night and barreled over several knights in the process.

Maybe I should've stayed, and simply died in the defense of the city. I will see, one day, if I was right to leave. But until then, I must live with my choice.

When we'd gotten some distance from the city, we found the knights had given up pursuit. Many of them hadn't had their horses as they swarmed the city on foot. But there was one group of knights who had found me – led by one very important man.

I watched Raymond's approach and quickly asked the brotherhood to hide as I faced down my mentor. I would've fled, but Raymond galloped towards me with no hostility. In fact, he wore a smile.

I readied myself for battle, even so.

"Easy, Julien," Raymond called as pulled up close to me. Behind him, Antioch was ablaze, and I heard distant, nightmare screams. "I was looking for you." His smile persisted.

"Here I am," I said confidently, though I could barely hide how rattled I was.

"Yes. Here you are. You seem to have found yourself, after all this time."

"No thanks to you."

Raymond's smile dipped. "I made you, Julien. Everything you're wearing – your armor and shield, and your weapon too – it belongs

191

to my army. Without me, you are nothing."

"You're wrong," I cried. "With you, I lost myself. I lost everything." I took a long, anxious breath. "Sir Raymond, I am not the man you made. I am Julien Allais, and I'm proud of the choices I made – the ones you stood against. I've found where I belong, and it's not here. I have someone to return to – someone important to me." I looked intently into his eyes. "This is goodbye… Raymond." I turned my horse and prepared to set off.

"You think you get to leave?" Raymond suddenly screamed. "After what you did – no, you don't get to walk away from this, Julien. All you deserve is death, and the fires of hell."

I glared at him, and growled. "So, what, you'll slaughter me, just like all those innocent people?"

Raymond laughed. It was an odd, kind of crazed laugh. "You never did understand. Well, I'm going to show you the truth, once and for all. But not here. You're going to Jerusalem, aren't you?"

"I am," I said firmly. "And Raymond – I will defend it from you."

"Good. Well, then, my boy, expect no mercy. We will bring that city down, too. And when I stand across from you next, I will kill you."

"I'm not afraid of you," I said shakily. Raymond grinned.

From somewhere in the shadows, Ahtmar whispered, "Julien… get ready to flee."

The brotherhood launched a wave of arrows at Raymond and his knights, killing most of them instantly. Raymond protected himself with his shield, and his armor saved his lower half.

In another burst of fire, Ahtmar and Hilal killed the remaining four warriors, which left Raymond alone.

"You dare even speak of mercy?" Ahtmar raged towards the knight. "Know this: you'll get none from us either!"

With that, we wheeled and retreated. Raymond would have to organize a group to chase after us, but his forces were short on horses – we got away without knights on our tail.

Raymond had burned Ahtmar's camp and killed his friends – the clash was inevitable. But I had become part of that conflict, and I was set to face my mentor again at Jerusalem. All things led there, different journeys, and different destinies – everything converged on that day.

Chapter 17

With Adhemar's map and Naasir's guidance, we raced towards Jerusalem. We pushed through exhaustion for an extra day to make sure we were a step ahead of Raymond. Our path to the holy land had become straightforward down the coast. In the summertime, the sea breeze had been a blessing, but in the winter it made the nights frigid and bitter.

When everyone in our group was utterly spent, we made camp for the night. The sounds of wood crackling and the gentle waves filled my ears. We all settled around the fire, and Hilal recommended we find some way to celebrate. We settled for a meal, the nicest we managed in the circumstances, and the gray commander tried to raise our spirits.

"Take heart," he said, which lifted each of the brotherhood's heads. "What we've been through – no one should ever have to endure. We've seen more death than anyone should." The brotherhood somberly agreed. "But sometimes, God's path is unclear to His struggling children." He stood, and he glowed orange against the flames. "We've spent many moons wondering, 'is this right?' 'Is this the path that we should walk?'" Our mood dipped, but Hilal tensed a fist and stood proudly. "I have an answer to that question."

"What answer?" Ahtmar sadly said.

"It is meant to be. Out of the fire, we rose. We endured. We survived. And through it all, we believed, so that we might make it to the holy city. Every road leads there, and there, everything will be revealed."

We'd all shared similar dreams, but to hear it spoken so confidently, after everything we'd faced together, was heartening.

Most of the brave brotherhood summoned a cheer, and a powerful "aye" that echoed through the darkness around us. Everyone but Ahtmar.

That night, he asked to be alone, and he let me take guard duty. It meant a lot that he trusted me to do it.

I sat near the fire and tried to stay awake. Before long, I had to stand to avoid falling asleep. I moved to the beach and looked out across the glimmering, moon-lit water. The wind was perfectly still. I felt like I was in a dream.

I turned back towards camp and blew my frosty breath into my hands, which were cold even with my gloves on.

Zahra walked towards me, wrapped in a colorful blanket. She waved.

"Hi, Zahra," I said. "Hey, you should be by the fire! What're you doing up, anyway?"

She stopped a few feet away from me. Perhaps, in another world, at another time, we might have shared something – an embrace.

But that was not to be. That was not part of Zahra's beautiful beliefs, to be with me there and then. And for me, it was the realization – again – that sacrifice was part of faith.

It was a part of love, too.

196

Instead, Zahra offered me another gift – the gift of words.

"I never got to thank you," she said. I listened eagerly. "You've been nothing but kind and generous towards us. After everything that's happened, you continue to stand up for us. You risked your life to save mine, and my brother's too. You fought for us time and time again when you never had to."

I smiled slightly, and Zahra smiled back. She had a smile that could change the world. "I care for you, Zahra," I managed to say as my heart raced.

"I care for you, too."

I took a big breath. "You know… I've been thinking for a long time about what my purpose is – why I'm here now." She tilted her head slightly. "I didn't know until recently. But with you here right now, I'm certain."

Zahra watched me with eyes that gleamed with knowledge and sparkled with hope. Her presence alone gave me strength and made me believe that anything was possible.

"I would like to be by your side, Zahra," I finally said. "Wherever that takes me."

Zahra swayed back and forth slowly. "I want that too, Julien."

"I'm so happy to hear you say that. Happier than I can say." I paused. "Zahra… you carry a light with you, wherever you go. It has guided me towards the truth at every turn. If I stay close to you, I know I'll find the right path."

She avoided my eyes. "I would like to tell Ahtmar how I feel about you." Her smile faded.

Suddenly, a chill ran through my spine. I felt terrified. I felt my strength leave me for a flash of a second. My eyes shot to our camp – to Ahtmar's tent. Had the flap moved? Was he watching us?

My moment with Zahra had been so pure, so wonderful. I

hadn't considered that her brother might've seen us. Even if we had simply spoken, a late-night, moonlit meeting would be the bane of any protective brother. But nothing happened. Things were quiet. I was still shaken.

"Are you okay, Julien?"

"I just had a bad feeling that Ahtmar saw us... and I'm realizing how difficult it's going to be to explain this to him."

She turned to look towards camp. "He was exhausted. I don't think he'd wake up till the morning." She paused, and turned back to me. "But you're right. I'm not sure he would accept it if... if I told him I cared for you."

"I understand...I can see why he would feel that way."

"In our beliefs, it's my brother's choice to decide who I can be with." She paused. "This will be a challenge, for many reasons."

"I don't wish to disrespect your faith, Zahra."

"I know... I'll have to think about this." She stepped away from me, and my heart sunk. "Truly, this wouldn't be right for my faith anyway."

I nodded slowly. "Let's see where our prayers guide us. Is that all right?"

"Okay, Julien."

I tossed and turned the whole night.

———

The next morning, we continued on the path to the holy land. Ahtmar seemed distant. I couldn't help but worry that he had seen Zahra and I last night, but I was probably overthinking it.

For a while, our journey became quiet. Days passed, and chilly nights went by in the blink of an eye. We made a brief stop at a port town, Tripoli, and stocked up on food and water.

I hadn't had the chance to speak with Zahra in a while, and that bothered me. She might've been right about Ahtmar – and we still hid our feelings from him. I wondered if I should face him, but I had been afraid – I didn't want to hurt him. And I suppose I didn't want him to hurt me, either.

Perhaps, like we had before, we could meet somewhere in the middle.

Our travel continued for weeks, and I sought every chance to talk with Zahra. The most I managed was a few minutes here and there, a handful of smiles and pleasantries. I was rarely given guard duty for the nights, and that only fed into my worries and suspicion more.

Things in Anatolia began to warm up again as we made it through the winter. I had a self-centered reflection one morning. It's like the heat was rising to signal that we're getting closer to Jerusalem. It was silly, but it was the kind of thing I pondered during the difficult, non-stop travel.

One spring night, my prayers were answered. I had a chance to be together with Zahra. She had convinced Ahtmar to rest.

It was a mild evening, with a nearly full moon that peeked through the clouds. I climbed to a low tree branch and sat there, and a misty breeze washed over me as I rocked my legs slowly back and forth.

"Hey," Zahra whispered from below, "what are you doing up there?"

"Hey there," I replied. "I'm just thinking."

"About what?"

"Everything. How we're going to talk to your brother. The possibility of going to war with my former mentor. What Jerusalem will be like. Will it be the way I imagine it? I have a thousand questions and no answers."

"That's life for you," she replied. "It's not all bad though, is it?"

She made me smile. "No, you have a point there. In fact, it's quite nice right now." I grabbed onto the tree and slid down.

Zahra was dressed in black., I understood and appreciated, her clothes and the veil that covered much of her head. They were a wonderful part of her beliefs.

We walked over to the water, and we made sure there was the cover of nature between us and camp to mask our meeting.

"How is your brother doing?" I picked up a rock and tossed it into the water. "I haven't spoken to him in a while."

When I looked at Zahra, the moonlight reflected in her sad eyes. Eventually, she said, "I think he's worried. I think he's feeling the same things we are about going to Jerusalem. And... I'm still not sure what to say to him about you."

"You don't think he suspects us, do you?"

"I think he would talk to me if he did. I've been trying to reach out to him, but it's been more difficult than it usually is. He's been through a lot, though..."

"Yes, that's true. We all have."

"There will be a time for it. I believe that."

"I'm glad." I tossed another rock, and it skipped along the surface of the water. "You know, there's something else I've been thinking about."

"What's that?"

"Well, I'm not the practical type." I mustered a quick laugh. "But I want to learn to use a bow. In the last battle, I could only use my shield."

Zahra smiled. "Give me a minute."

She snuck into her tent and returned with a bow and a quiver of arrows in hand. She handed the bow to me.

"You can use one?" I asked with my mouth slightly open.

"Is that so strange? Anyway, I don't use it often. Ahtmar wants me avoiding battles, no matter what."

"I see. Well, I might say I feel the same about that."

Zahra looked disappointed. "What if I could help you?"

I frowned. "Do you want to?"

"No. But I may have to."

I sighed deeply. "I wouldn't turn away your help, Zahra."

She nodded. I checked out the bow. I flipped it over a few times, and then held it with both hands. Zahra tossed me an arrow. She walked over to a nearby tree and marked a circular spot in the wood with the tip of another arrow.

"Go ahead," she said. "Take aim."

I held the bow up, and Zahra verbally corrected my stance. I held my arms out farther apart than I initially had, spread my feet a little, and made my hands level.

"That's about it," she said. "Now just relax."

"All right," I replied with a quick breath.

"Try to close one eye to help with your aim."

I did so and kept my hands steady as I focused on the point she marked. The moonlight made it clear, but I still struggled, and Zahra noticed that.

"My parents told me something interesting, when they first trained me," she said. "They said when you fire a bow like this, where you hit determines where your mind is. If you fire short, you're stuck in the past. Too high, and you're worrying about the future."

"And the center?"

"Well, then you're living life the ideal way – purely in the present. It's something I've tried to be mindful of."

My hands shook slightly as I focused more intently. I took a deep breath and let the arrow loose. To my surprise, I actually hit the tree – but I hit some fifteen feet higher than the mark.

"So, Julien," Zahra said as she walked closer to me. "Do you believe in the story?" I looked down sadly. Zahra raised my head by saying, "We can make it through this."

"You're wonderful, Zahra…"

We watched the water for a while longer. We contemplated and wondered. We both weren't certain if our connection was right – if it was meant to be. But my heart and spirit guided me towards her.

"Zahra… I want to see this journey through, but I think the only way I can is with you beside me."

She stared sadly out at the sea. "Not long ago, I realized… no one would accept it. My brother won't. With my faith and my beliefs – this shouldn't be." My heart ached. "In a way, your faith is the same. You were sent to destroy us – to destroy the Turks."

"No," I firmly said. Zahra looked at me. I thought back to Peter's words – and Raymond's. It was true. Zahra, Ahtmar, and all of the Turks I'd met were supposed to be my mortal enemies. I shook my head. "I can't separate from my faith. But… there is something deep in my soul that can see a greater truth." I gazed at the heavens before I looked back at Zahra. "If God did send me here – it was to meet you. To be with you."

Zahra's eyes glimmered like the stars above. She giggled. "Well, I wasn't quite finished, you know… I care for you too, and I want to be by your side."

My heart jumped. "Really?"

"Yes… but I will have to pray. I will have to continue to speak with Allah, to find peace, to find answers."

"Zahra… thank you."

202

I slept peacefully that night, but in the back of my mind, a shred of doubt ate away at me, like a dark whisper.

Our journey resumed, and I took the opportunity to train my skills with a bow. Hilal was kind enough to offer me a spare. He even practiced with me. Every spare hour I had, usually before bed, I fired arrows into targets the same way Zahra had showed me. I missed each and every time, but I also got a little closer.

Soon enough, we arrived at another port city, Jaffa. It was small, but impressive in how busy it was. Workers shouted as they hauled goods on and off the dozens of docked ships. A nervous energy emanated from the city. Something seemed amiss, but I couldn't put a finger on it. We needed more supplies, so Ahtmar went inside with Naasir and most of the brotherhood. They left Hilal with Zahra and I. The heaven-sent girl hopped off of Hilal's horse and approached mine, just in time to calm my nerves.

"Hi, Julien." She patted my horse's side. "How are you? And how is your horse?"

I smiled. "I'm good, and she is too. She's strong for her size—" I whispered, "—kind of like you."

Zahra giggled. "Still no name for her, huh?"

"No. It's about time we change that, isn't it?"

"Yes. I have an idea for her. Try and pronounce it first, okay? Ready?" I nodded, and she continued, "Jisra."

"It sounds nice. Jisra."

"Not bad, but give it another try. Jees-rah. Got it?"

"Jees-rah. I think I got it."

"Good." She whispered, "Jisra is our word for bridge. It's what you are, Julien, and what my brother is – a bridge between beliefs."

"Thank you, Zahra…"

We naively stared at one another before Hilal drew my attention.

"I can tell, you know," he quietly said as he fed his horse. "Most of the others – they're tired, beaten down. They can't see it like I can."

I trotted closer to him, and Zahra followed.

"You two care for each other." He frowned. "You should just come out and say it."

"Is it that obvious...?" Zahra asked.

"Oh, come on. And if you think your brother doesn't know, you'd be foolish. He's... affected by it."

"Oh, no..." I muttered. "I just want to handle it right... I don't want to disrespect him."

Around this time a large group of Seljuks headed our way. They stocked crates outside the gates and called for horses. Their tones were frightened.

Hilal continued, "The way you two have danced around with glances and smiles... you're trying to keep it a secret. How much more disrespectful can you be to him?"

Zahra weaved around the horse and stepped up to the gray commander. "He promised me I could introduce someone to him, but... I know he's not ready."

"And you think that makes it all right to do this? To hide the truth?"

"No, I..."

"Something's wrong, Zahra." Hilal kneeled before her, and pleaded, "Can't you see it? Your brother is not well."

"What do you mean...?"

"His passion – his fire – it's gone. When I look at him now, he has this faraway stare in his eyes, this emptiness that... it hurts my very soul." Hilal peered out towards the frantic city.

"I know he's been distant lately, but... how have I not seen it?" Zahra held her hands together tightly. "Brother..."

My stomach was in knots. I had no answers, but I did find another question. "Can we do anything to help him?"

"You need to be honest with him," Hilal said. "Tell him the truth. We need him. There is still much we have to do."

"All right. Zahra, if you're okay with it, I am too."

"Sure..." She glanced at the ground.

"And Zahra," Hilal continued, "you'd best think about if this is right – this relationship. Is this what Allah would want?"

Before Zahra answered, Ahtmar and the brotherhood stormed out of the city. They approached one of the men who had just dropped a heavy crate onto the stockpile.

"Peace be upon you, brother!" Ahtmar called. "Why are the men leaving the city in such a hurry?"

"Peace be upon you," came the nervous reply. "Well... wait, who's asking? You're not a spy, are you?"

"If he was," Naasir said, "you'd probably be in deep trouble already. But we're not – what kind of spy do you mean?"

"The Fatimid. They've claimed this area."

"Wait a minute," Ahtmar said as he climbed off his horse. "What are you talking about? The Fatimid have what area?"

I'd heard the name before – Fatimid – I faintly remembered from Jean's lessons, which felt ancient to me. Back then, I never questioned him on the difference between Seljuk and Fatimid – I was too foolish – but I knew it was something important.

The Seljuk guard looked exasperated. He heaved another heavy crate into the stockpile nearby and continued, "They took Jerusalem. It's no longer in Seljuk hands."

"They stole the holy land from us? When?"

"Not long ago. How didn't you know that? Are you traveling from the north?"

"Yes – we were heading to Jerusalem."

"It's a lost cause. The Fatimid have seen to that. And that's not the worst part."

"The knights." Ahtmar slowly ran his hands down his face.

"Yes. We got word today from a ship that came in. We're not getting caught in the middle of the war. We're leaving."

"Where will you go…?" I asked.

The soldier looked at me, wide eyed. "Who's this? You captured one of the knights?"

"Never mind him," Ahtmar said. "Why are you leaving? There are hundreds of soldiers here – we could use you in the fight."

"We know when a war is lost, my friend. You should know the rest of the news, then – the knights beat back a joint Seljuk effort at Antioch."

"I know. We were there."

"The initial loss was terrible enough, but this happened afterwards."

Ahtmar was visibly shaken. Zahra approached him and placed a hand on his arm. "What in the world do you mean…?"

"All of the Seljuk leaders met to topple the knights after they captured Antioch. And they failed – completely. There's no one left to stop those silver monsters… the only ones that may have a chance are the Fatimid."

"Is there truly no hope…?" Ahtmar's voice was tortured with emotion.

"Not for the Turks." The man continued gathering supplies, and Jaffa became more desolate with every passing minute.

"We have to go," Ahtmar firmly said. "Now."

"Ahtmar…" I quietly replied. "We can do something about this – together." He didn't seem to hear what I said. The whole

206

brotherhood felt like we had sunk into the dirt and sand around us, like we carried the world on our shoulders. And maybe we had.

"Let's move." Ahtmar paused and quietly added, "What has happened to Jerusalem...?"

Just when Zahra and I had prepared to share the news of our relationship, we took off in a hurry. I was in a cold sweat as we rode on towards the holy city. With Raymond behind us, and an unknown enemy in Jerusalem, my mind was thrown into chaos.

Chapter 18
A few days later

I followed the weakened brotherhood towards Jerusalem at a frenzied pace.

Every night we made camp, I prayed – I asked God to offer guidance, and answers. Most of all, I prayed for the safety of every one of us – including Ahtmar. More and more, the boy who was a reflection of me transformed. He was becoming more distant and more troubled. With the weight of my secret on my mind, I had been unable to work up the courage to tell him the truth, and he had seemed to have grown to resent me for it. Just as we were caught between two armies, Ahtmar and I were trapped in a divide of unwillingness to meet the other, to be the one to first extend a hand.

I should have gone to him.

One night, everyone else was asleep except for the two of us. Ahtmar had just finished guard duty, and I was set to take his place. As we passed each other, we accidentally bumped shoulders, and we both spun to face one another. We finally made eye contact after what felt like weeks.

The moment was there, to finally shine the light of truth on the secret, but my weakness persisted. Ahtmar waited – he just waited there, stared, and expected me to say it, but I didn't. I did speak, but I confronted another truth instead.

"How are you doing, Ahtmar?" I pointlessly asked. He said nothing. "I... I wanted to ask you something." Again, he waited. "When you brought me into your group, you said something that stuck with me."

Ahtmar raised his head.

"You said you wanted to reveal the truth to me about your faith – about Islam. You wish for me to become a Muslim?"

The boy took a strong step forward. "I cannot force you to see the light of truth. But if you cannot choose to see it yourself – to see how terrible things are because of your faith, then I don't know what to say to you."

"Wait," I quickly replied. "That's not fair. That's –" The boy cut me off and stepped towards me again.

"What's not fair is everything that your people have done to the Turks. What they've done to the Christians." He hesitated for a flash of a moment, and then he shoved me. I stumbled back. "What's not fair is what you've done, Julien. At every turn, you pulled away from us – you even returned to your army and allowed them to slaughter the people of Antioch."

"I didn't allow it!" I snapped. "I did everything in my power to stop them. What else could I have done?"

"You could've taken Raymond's head," he shouted. By now, the brotherhood had stirred awake. "You could've fought..." Tears welled in the boy's eyes.

I took a big, shaky breath as I barely held back my own emotion. "I would've died, and then, I couldn't help you anymore. I couldn't be here, right now, to go to Jerusalem with you." Ahtmar shook his head, but I persisted, "I want to be here. More than anything."

"Then tell me the truth," he shouted, and pushed me onto my back. I stared up at him, and my tears fell just as his did. The brotherhood moved in to separate us, and Zahra watched with her hands in prayer.

"Would you accept it?" I weakly said.

The boy's face was marked with pain, with disappointment, and my heart truly ached. I couldn't tell him, even if I had in a way.

Our next days were a blur as we pushed on against the hot spring wind. I hardly slept and endured fresh nightmares each night. The fear of losing Zahra, and a friend in Ahtmar, ate away at my soul.

He didn't fare any better. Any time I shot awake from a dark dream, he would be there. He stared blankly, darkly into the distance.

After another day on the road, I saw Ahtmar approach his sister late in the evening. With the dusk sun at his back, he asked her to be truthful with him — to tell him what she hid. He told her he was the only one who loved her, who could protect her, but she only repeated, "yes, brother." She held the truth deep inside, just like I did.

After three days of nearly non-stop travel, the dawn shone brightly. We were tired, but the energy in camp quickly rose. We were close to Jerusalem. Both Zahra and I avoided Ahtmar, and I sensed his boiling frustration. His unhappiness squirmed and twisted. Solemnly, he got on his horse, and Zahra quietly joined him. The brotherhood was ready to ride, so we set out.

Only a couple of hours passed when we came to a large ridge. We scaled upwards, and I pressed Jisra more than I ever had. She was exhausted. At the top, silence fell among us.

Below, far on the horizon, was the holy city of Jerusalem. The temples and buildings, and what could've been the Dome of the

Rock were visible from here. Everything seemed to glimmer with light, with radiant energy. It stood out like a beacon among the sand and dirt.

My heart raced, and my feelings swelled and ascended into joy.

Ahtmar said, "So this is the city where the prophet ascended to heaven… peace be upon Him…"

"This is where the Lord died," I said, "and returned to life…" Our tired, broken group was completely overcome with emotion.

Zahra grabbed onto her brother tightly and leaned over to whisper to him. I faintly heard them from here. "It's so beautiful, brother. It's magical. I… I'm so sorry I've been keeping things from you. Once we get to safety, I'll explain everything. For now, I want to celebrate this moment. We made it."

"Zahra… this is an amazing day indeed. I love you, sister."

"I love you, too." She squeezed him tightly.

I found a resurgence of hope, like I had been wrapped in its light.

Despite the transcendent wonder of Jerusalem, it was surrounded by imposing stone walls – what looked to be two layers. There were multiple gates. At least two for any entrance to the city. They were all defended from the walls. And if the rumors were true, we would have no friends here.

Something was happening outside the city. Hundreds of people were leaving, and they formed a long stream. They were no warriors. I saw no weapons of any kind.

"My brothers, let's make for the gates – it's time to see what awaits us."

"Aye!" everyone shouted, including me.

We raced down the ridge, back to the main road towards the city. We were on course to pass the swath of people, but they hardly paid attention to us as we rushed past them. As we made it to the end of their line, Ahtmar slowed down and called to them.

A few turned back. They looked dejected. One man replied, "What do you want?"

"What's happened? Why is there an exodus from the holy city?"

"The Fatamid forced us out. You didn't know? You lot look like you'd be part of their forces."

"Us? You mean you're all Christians?"

"Yes. They said we were a risk – something about an army heading this way."

"How were things in the city?" I asked. "What were the Turks doing before?" The question was the last bit of my naivety being expelled, like some demonic spirit. I already knew the answer. I already knew that Raymond, Adhemar, and the pope had been dead wrong about Jerusalem under Turkish rule, but I suppose I still had to hear it.

Some ten more peasants paused to listen. "What are you asking?" the man continued. "If the Muslims treated us poorly? Don't make me laugh. Jerusalem was a home to all religions. It was a place of relative peace – until now."

I nodded slowly and frowned.

"Are you surprised, Julien?" Ahtmar glared at me. "Your march here was founded on lies."

"Easy, brother…" Zahra patted his arm.

"I know, Ahtmar," I said sadly. "I'm sorry."

The boy turned back to the peasant. "Thank you for the information. Good luck."

The massive group continued onwards – wherever they were going.

We hurried to the gates, leaving a trail of dust and dirt that crackled behind us. Guards swarmed around the walls and took aim at us. They were a mixed group, with red and brown light armors, but they seemed united in targeting us. One soldier in black, with a turban wrapped around his helmet, called off the archers.

"Peace be upon you," he said. "Who are you? What are you doing here?"

"Peace be upon you, friend," Ahtmar replied. "We're pilgrims. We hope to find peace here."

"Is that right? You don't look like pilgrims to me. You look like Seljuks." He paused. "If you plan to reclaim the city, it's pointless. There's another force headed this way that plans to throw everyone out."

"That's not our goal," Ahtmar maintained. "What you see before you are the remains of a Seljuk clan – and one former member of the approaching army. All of us have seen enough war to last a lifetime. We wish to find guidance inside Jerusalem."

"That sounds noble – but I don't see any reason to trust you."

"I have family inside the city!" Naasir shouted. "I'm part of the Shaheen family – we have holy duties at one of the mosques. Would that be enough to let us in?"

The guards above debated amongst themselves in hushed tones. The leader responded, "We'll investigate that. In the meantime, you should get comfortable. We're busy preparing for war – I can't guarantee anything."

"We don't have time to wait out here!" Ahtmar raged. "The knights are coming, and they won't just kill you – they'll kill every innocent person inside! Let us help you!"

"We're not convinced of that. You'll wait – or perish trying to break in." He turned to leave but stopped for a moment. "Oh, I can offer you some advice in the meantime. Don't drink from any of the wells outside – we've already made sure the invaders can't use them when they arrive." He walked away.

Ahtmar's anger trembled, and his body shook. If affected us all. After we waited agonizing hours, the heat had pressed down on us, and our vision was hazy, so Ahtmar decided we had to make camp. We set up near the few trees, about a half-mile away, and used whatever shade we could as shelter from the sun.

Ahtmar sat outside my tent while the rest of the brotherhood kept their sword arms warm. Naasir cursed under his breath with every wild swing. Zahra and I kept our distance from Ahtmar and each other for a while, but we gradually moved closer. Ahtmar lit a small fire and sat back, and he looked up to the heavens. Eventually, Zahra and I joined him around the flame.

We knew we couldn't hide the truth any longer – and I wonder now if being locked out of Jerusalem had been the sign to prove it.

"So," Zahra said, timidly. "Ahtmar."

"Go ahead," he replied. His head fell forward into his hands, and after a moment he lifted it. "Do you know how long I've waited?"

"Brother... I'm sorry. Well..."

"Ahtmar," I firmly said. He snapped to attention. "I've been disrespectful to you. I apologize for that. I didn't want to hurt your feelings – but I realize now that I went about this completely the wrong way." I paused with a quick breath. My heart raced out of control. "Zahra means a great deal to you, but I've found something out during our time together. She means a lot to me too."

He stared at me and listened.

"I've gotten to know her, and I wanted to tell you – she has guided me through this journey. She has helped me to question my choices, but more than that, she helped me see the truth."

We both looked at his sister. She wore a bright, positive, hopeful smile. "I've never seen that expression from you, Zahra," Ahtmar said. He glanced at me. "But she has that ability – to light the way. She has always been a guiding star."

"Yes," I calmly said. "But… if she wants to be in a relationship – that's your choice to make." Ahtmar's eyes turned harsh. "That was the other reason why we kept this secret – we felt you might not let her do that."

"You speak as if you know her," he replied as he leaned forward. "But you don't. You fell into our lap like an abandoned child, only a short time ago. I am her only family. I've known her my entire life." He pointed at me. "And you – the first time you met us, you killed our friends and burned our camp! So what do you know?"

"Brother!" Zahra cried. "That's not true! He's only helped us, and he's stood against his allies every time. But… I realized you wouldn't accept him. How could I approach you knowing you'd just turn me down? I care for Julien, deeply, and that is my feeling."

Ahtmar faced Zahra. "Why would you grow fond of a man who sought to kill us all? Who clearly can't accept our faith – who holds onto the faith of those other murderers? How can we be sure he won't go back to them?"

"I would never betray you," I said. "Never again. I swear that on my life."

"No? Then what if I challenged you –what if I asked you to consider Islam?"

I got to my feet, and Ahtmar moved to his in response. Zahra looked on with sadness in her eyes.

I firmly said, "I've believed in my faith since I was a child. I hold it deeply in my soul, as absolute truth."

"Where has that truth led you, Julien?" Ahtmar snapped. "It has led to a graveyard of victims, whose numbers grow every single day. And when that truth gets here – to the holy land – it will leave behind this world's greatest wound." Ahtmar narrowed his eyes and cried, "That is your absolute truth!"

I shouted in anger and punched him. He slammed to the earth. As he stormed back to his feet, I grabbed my sword handle, and he grabbed his.

I knew I was wrong. But I couldn't accept Ahtmar's proposition, even if he had done it to help me, to guide me. My faith was as important to me as his was to him – and despite having called him my friend, that was a fact that made our clash almost impossible to avoid.

We had both been lost – so lost that we couldn't see the bridge between beliefs that we had both already created.

"I can't do it, Ahtmar," I weakly said. "I can't. And as much as I'd like you to see the joys of my faith, I can't ask you to change either. But you're my friend, Ahtmar. Doesn't that mean anything?"

"You don't know me," he barked. "And you don't know Zahra!"

The brotherhood had heard our skirmish and moved in to protect us – both of us. They had been what held us together, but there was little left to prevent our connection from being shattered, right outside the holy land.

As the brotherhood consoled Ahtmar, the two of us remained locked in each other's gaze, as we were on our first fated meeting, where we had been surrounded by hellfire.

Zahra went to her brother's side and rubbed his jaw. She peered at me sadly, and then at him. "Brother… can't we just live with our differences, at least for now? We're right outside Jerusalem."

"What if we can't get in?" he asked. "What if this is the end – and there's no hope?"

"Then we should pray here," I muttered. "We should seek answers together. I know this might not mean the same thing to you – to your beliefs – but I was taught that the kingdom of heaven lies within. We should look there."

Ahtmar exhaled shakily. Zahra's sadness eventually swayed him to an agreement. "Fine. Tonight, we rest and pray."

Zahra smiled through tear-filled eyes.

Hilal stepped up to his leader. "You're not alone," he said. "We'll stand with you until the end. Don't lose sight of that, my friend. All right?"

"Stand tall, Ahtmar," Naasir added. "And stand proud. We are survivors. We'll make it."

Ahtmar looked at each of his loyal men intently and bowed his head. The whole of the brotherhood pressed their fists into their chests in solidarity. Their faces were sullen and tired, but I knew they believed in their leader. That had been just enough to push us onwards.

———

The night came with no envoys from the city. Ahtmar sent men there every hour and made a larger fire so they could see us, but Jerusalem remained silent.

Zahra and I headed to Ahtmar's sandy tent. Slowly, hesitantly, we opened the flap and stepped inside.

"Hi, Ahtmar," Zahra said. She smiled as she moved next to her brother. I settled on the opposite side of him.

I attempted to smile the way Zahra did. I tried to capture her light and shine it on Ahtmar. It probably came across as a cheap imitation. "I meant what I said before," I said. "I want to pray, but only if we all do it. I believe there's power in praying together."

"All right," Ahtmar quietly replied. Outside, the brotherhood grouped up near the tent, and soon joined in prayer – in what I learned was actually called salah. The preparations, the elegant motions, the careful, precise movements, and the bright energies I felt were overwhelmingly beautiful. For a while, I was a simple observer – in stunned appreciation of what salah was, and what it meant to the people who embraced it.

The unity sent a spark through my heart, and I think it did the same for Ahtmar. The boy expressed a smile, the first true, wonderful smile that I'd seen in a long time. Maybe there really is something to this, I thought. Maybe we can finally work things out.

They faced south, in the direction of the Kaaba, their holiest place of worship.

When I was able to focus, I offered my own prayers. I simply sat on my knees with my hands together. I wished for peace to reign, for everyone here, everyone in Jerusalem, and even for the knights on their way. They might not have deserved it, but I wished they would turn away, and see their mistakes naked in the sun.

My whole body tensed up tightly. My spirit spoke to me, telling me that something so joyous was not set for my future.

But I persisted. We all persisted and prayed for divine guidance from the heavens. As Zahra and I completed our rituals, I noticed Ahtmar still knelt. Then, after a while, he rose with his hands on his knees. His expression broke my heart. He was a ghost.

Still, he turned to his sister and they both said, "Allah is most great," in unison. The brotherhood spoke the same thing outside to one another.

Things fell quiet, and a light rain began to patter against the tent. I watched Ahtmar, and I wondered what he was thinking. I wondered how I could free him from his suffering, and truly, if he could free me from mine – as friends.

Moments later, the siblings completed their salah. "Peace and blessings of Allah be unto you," they repeated to each other.

Ahtmar then turned and said the same to me. I happily said, "Thank you, Ahtmar. And may the Lord bless you."

Zahra and I both found a smile. Mine dipped as I felt Ahtmar's eyes on me. They were so cold, so dark. I simply told him, "I'm here for you, my friend. No matter what. We can make it through this, together."

He nodded by barely tilting his chin down.

Zahra and I both thanked him again, and then we headed out to join the brotherhood. Like us, they were inspired by the prayer, and we greeted each other warmly. Naasir and Hilal even hugged me, which left my mouth open in surprise. I returned their gesture, but it was after my embrace with Hilal that I realized something was truly wrong.

"Your heart is racing," the elder Turk told me. "What's the matter? Battle has not found us just yet."

"I don't... I don't know..." As we separated, I pressed a hand to my chest, and felt my heart pounding uncontrollably. And that was when I looked back towards the tent. Ahtmar was staring at me.

His face was that of a man who our dark world had claimed. A man who the toll of war, the loss of loved ones, and the threat of destruction at the hands of vicious monsters had stripped away all of his hope.

And I think, what had been almost unbelievable to me, was that I hadn't become that same man. The only thing that might've preserved my life – my will – was Zahra. And she was the same person who Ahtmar felt he had lost – because of me.

I couldn't stop what was to come, but that night, I told myself I would do everything in my power to protect the two people who mattered most to me.

Chapter 19

Raymond was fast approaching, and the gates of Jerusalem remained closed to us. We rested overnight, restored our strength, and in the morning we were set to make our final attempt to enter the city.

Our group raced towards the gates. Ahtmar trailed behind us. When we approached, we waited for him to speak to the guards, but he didn't. Zahra whispered something to him that I couldn't hear. Something was wrong.

Naasir took the initiative instead. "Please – we mean you no harm. We wish to find peace in the city – and we'll stave off the knights alongside you to do it!"

I squinted to see some of the men on the walls. The leader was definitely the same man we had first spoken to. He frantically pointed and directed warriors around the walls. Eventually, he responded to us.

"You're back? I thought you'd have fled by now. The invaders will be here any second."

I had to do something to get us inside. I was worried about Ahtmar. The fear had crept up my spine and twisted my body into a knot of anxiety. If we could enter the holy city, I believed we could find time to speak.

"Hello up there!" I shouted. "My name is Julien. Please, listen – I know some of the men who are marching this way. I can assure you that they intend to kill you – all of you. If you let us in, we can help defend the city!"

"How could we possibly trust you?" The Fatimid commander folded his arms. "It's unexpected that you speak my language, but you just admitted you're part of their army!"

"I'm not. Not anymore. I saw how terribly wrong they were, and now Jerusalem is the only chance I have at finding the answers I seek. I promise you, we will fight by your side."

"You know nothing about us! I can't waste time with you anymore. I have a war to prepare for." He turned to walk away.

"Wait!" I managed to get his attention. "You're right – I do know nothing about you. But I've tried to learn your language, and I want to learn more. What's your name?"

He laughed, exasperated. "Qadi."

"I see. Qadi, wouldn't you rather have extra warriors defending this city? How could it possibly hurt?"

He groaned loudly. "Fine. If you submit your weapons to us, we'll let you in."

"I think that's fair." I turned to the brotherhood. Mostly everyone agreed, but Ahtmar remained quiet. His vacant stare persisted. I don't think he was listening. A cold sweat formed on my forehead.

The gates were dragged open with a loud clank. I saw temples and churches, along with men, women and children. They scrambled in preparation for the silver nightmare.

The brotherhood charged towards the gates, but Ahtmar was

frozen. Zahra patted his arm, and pleaded with him, but he said nothing. Our group turned back when they realized their leader had stayed behind.

"Ahtmar!" I cried. "What's going on? Let's get inside the city! We have no time to waste!"

After a long pause, he finally said something. "Julien, this can't go on any longer." He hopped off of his horse, and Zahra followed. He walked towards me. I decided to step down from Jisra as well.

"What, Ahtmar? What can't go on?"

"You. Being with us."

"But why…?"

"I lost everything. My family, my home, my friends, and now – the one thing I had left, the one single thing…" He peered at Zahra as his words faded. Then, he glared at me. "I brought you in, and you took her away."

"Ahtmar, I'm sorry…" My heart ached. The worst part was, he might've been right about me. I had gone about everything completely the wrong way. Zahra and I had connected in secret. We hid, and evaded, and deceived. I blamed myself.

Zahra approached her brother. She wrapped her arms around him, but he pulled away. The girl tried to move to him, but he continued towards me.

"Brother," Zahra called. "Please, stop this. You haven't lost me. You're everything to me."

"Your God showed me the meaning of brutality, Julien," Ahtmar firmly said as he ignored the girl's pleas. He sighed deeply, emotionally. In heartbreak. "I never should have brought you with us… Hell has followed us, trailing after you."

I felt his terrible, ill intent, and then, he drew his sword. I held my shield high in response. "This might surprise you, Ahtmar…

but I think you're right."

In spite of his rage, tears brimmed in his eyes.

"But even if that's true, I want you to know that... I'm still happy I came with you. I'm happy I got to know you."

Ahtmar said nothing, but his face – the mix of sadness and anger, of his spirit embattled against itself – crushed me. I had to set that aside. I had to endure his storm in order to let his sun break.

"I plan to fight for Jerusalem, Ahtmar. And I plan to fight for Zahra. If you hate me, that's fine. I would even understand that. But I can't die. Not yet. I want to live – for you."

"I have said it before," the boy darkly said. "I will do anything on this earth to preserve my sister's life. With you... she is doomed. So you, Julien – I deny you."

There was a long, unbearably tense moment as Ahtmar and I stood across from each other. Zahra moved in between us. She shifted her view from her brother, to me, back and forth. She ultimately realized this battle was going to happen. She stepped back and watched on in horror.

The wind rushed by and kicked up sand, which swirled in chaos.

"Ahtmar!" Hilal called. "Is there nothing we can do to stop you? We – your brothers – we're all here for you!" The brotherhood cheered, but they sounded like pleas.

His dark eyes were fixed upon me. He was deaf even to his allies. "There is no hope left," he said, "in this world, and in this life."

The implication sent chills of terror through me. But deep inside, I knew he didn't mean it. "You deserve to live, Ahtmar!"

Behind me, I heard the heavy gates of Jerusalem close. The Fatimid had understandably run out of patience. We were locked out. I wondered if our fates were sealed – if we would all die before we reached the holy land. I was left with only one thing to do: face down Ahtmar.

The boy sprinted towards me. He swung his sword quickly, and I had to use all my strength to deflect it with my shield. I brought my weapon up, but he was lightning fast. In the same moment, he slashed my arm. My armor absorbed most of the blow, but the pain rocked me. I used my shield and bashed him in the chest, and he stumbled back.

He persisted through his sister's cries. He dashed at me again. I held my shield up in desperate defense, but his speed was unlike anything I'd seen. In a blur, Ahtmar slammed his blade right into my injured shoulder. I hit the ground and writhed in pain. Ahtmar hovered over me.

He lifted his blade up, but he hesitated in ending my life. I found the strength to pull my shield up, and he decided to swing. The force crushed the wood into my gut. I gasped for air. Ahtmar kicked me in the jaw.

He attempted to kick me again, but I thrust my shield upwards and knocked him off of me. I rolled to my feet and breathed heavily as the air returned to my chest. Zahra shouted for us to stop, and the brotherhood echoed her pleas.

Ahtmar lunged at me again with a mighty swing. This time, I used his momentum against him. I rolled to the side, and he tumbled to the dirt. I jumped ahead and slashed his arm once. He cried out in pain. His black clothing was ripped, and the streak of red formed soon after.

He shifted to his hands and knees and threw off his helmet into the sand. He slowly stood and faced me again.

Then, I felt a vibration in my gut. The ground began to rumble beneath our feet. I gasped. The army was here? I snapped my head towards the road. On the far horizon, Raymond's army glimmered in the sun as they marched towards us. They were thousands, uncountable, but still – they were weakened. The numbers were diminished from what I remembered, even from when I last saw them at Antioch. I recalled what the man at the port had told us – about their battle against a massive Seljuk force. That may have been what cut their numbers.

The army slowed to a stop. Perhaps they had the same transcendent feeling we all did when we first saw Jerusalem. No matter what, our time was limited.

"Ahtmar," I shouted, "please – I care about you. Find your soul, your spirit – I know you're in there listening! There is more to do in this world!"

My last words caused the boy's head to recoil, as if they triggered something in his mind. But then, he whipped up his sword and slashed at me. I blocked with my shield, and we both struggled for control.

Meanwhile, the brotherhood begged the Fatimid to open the gates and let us inside. As I struggled against Ahtmar, I was yet again astonished by the kindness of the people I was taught to treat as enemies. The gates of Jerusalem were once again opened. Raymond's army was far enough away – and they had remained frozen as they observed the holy city in worship. That was perhaps the only thing that made it possible.

Ahtmar and I couldn't break through each other's guard. I had to do something – the most important thing I could think of at that moment. "Hilal!" I cried. "Take Zahra and get inside the city!"

"Aye!" he quickly responded. He and the brotherhood galloped to Zahra, and he picked her up onto his horse. She resisted every step of the way. She battered his arms, screamed, and tried to shake free.

As they made for the gates, I said one last thing: "Zahra… I love you!" Her tears fell sideways to the sand as she was pulled away.

"I love you, too!" she shouted. "Both of you! You… you damn fools!"

Her words summoned something else in Ahtmar. The life returned to his face, and his eyes burned with passion. He yelled, a battle roar, and shoved me back easily. My shield was knocked away, well out of reach. I narrowly dodged two more quick swings from my friend and returned the favor with one of my own. He blocked my blade easily, but I used my might and pushed his weapon back toward his body. We were deadlocked again, and that was when the Catholic army rumbled towards us.

"Get inside, dammit!" came a call from the walls. "We're shutting the gates!"

Ahtmar looked into my eyes deeply, while I maintained a fiery gaze. I believe he had searched for something in my very soul. Whatever he saw made him smile.

He swung around to the opposite side of me, with his back to the army. A hail of arrows rained down from the Catholic archers. Ahtmar shielded me. Tens of arrows pierced his body, his arms and legs. He collapsed onto me. I barely held him up, and I cried out in misery.

"It's all right," he managed to say. "This is what I wanted."

"What do you mean…?" I strained to hold him up.

"Don't worry about me. I must go. There is nothing left for me here."

"Ahtmar…" I hugged him. I looked down at his back and saw the jagged bolts sticking out. It crushed my heart.

"Protect Zahra, do you hear me? I know that you can. Save her from this dark world… please…"

"I will." I looked at the archers. They had prepared another wave. My life was preserved by the Fatamid – their defensive archers sent out a barrage, which pushed back the invaders for just a minute longer. I said to my friend, "One day, your people and mine will be able to sit down in peace. I believe that."

"Do you really…?"

"You allowed it, and so did I." I pulled back to look Ahtmar in the eyes. "Someday, it will happen."

"Good." His strength was all but gone. His smile faded. "Thank you, Julien."

"And thank you. Rest easy… my friend." Slowly, carefully, I let him down. He was still propped up by the arrows.

"Friend." He let out one last, quiet laugh, and then he whispered, "Yes… my friend…"

I grabbed my shield and raced to Jisra. I calmed her quickly, hopped on, and charged to the closing gates.

Zahra's hands covered her face, and she cried desperately. The brotherhood looked at me, solemnly, and each one held a fist to their chest. Together, we all hurried inside Jerusalem, and the gates slammed shut behind us.

Our hearts were heavy, but there was no time to mourn. We left our horses by the stone stairs and made for the walls. We were surrounded by unknown Fatimid soldiers, but at that moment, we had been unquestionably allies.

I saw Ahtmar from here. A wave of knights charged up to him on their horses. They viciously ran him through.

"God damn you!" I yelled. Zahra shrieked and took aim with her own bow. She nailed an arrow into a knight's back as he retreated, but it bounced right off of his armor.

Hilal tossed me a bow. I held it up along with the rest of the brotherhood. But the army hadn't continued towards us. They had cruelly claimed their victim outside the gates, so they began to surround Jerusalem.

I narrowed my focus to just the well-armored knights. I sought out some of the leaders, and I quickly found Raymond. As the knights split into groups, I noticed Tancred and Godfrey, but I hadn't seen Bohemond or bishop Adhemar. I wasn't concerned for the giant, but Adhemar might've been the only one who could've talked sense into the others. I had a sinking feeling in my gut. He had been sick at Antioch… did he not survive?

The army kept their distance and marched in a circle around the city. It might've been an attempt to scare us, to force us to surrender, but when I looked closely, I saw that the men marched barefoot. It must be some form of penance, I thought. They must be feeling what I did when I first laid eyes on this city…

We remained at the ready, but the army settled in. They planned to besiege us. I turned to Qadi, who was beside us on the wall.

"What do you think our chances are?" I asked.

He frowned. "We… didn't expect this kind of army. We had just kicked the Turks out, and were preparing to resupply Jerusalem, but that hasn't happened yet. Our forces here are only a portion of the men we're facing." He glanced at me. "But we will fight until the end."

I took a heavy breath and looked behind me, at the unreal, ascendant city that was set to be attacked. What I'd wanted then was to take a journey with Zahra – to explore the fabled holy sites that were part of my faith, and the faith of my love. Places like the Temple Mount, the three sacred mosques of Islam, and the Holy Sepulcher, where Jesus' tomb was supposed to lie.

But the knights had taken that opportunity away. There was

hardly time for anything but fear and terror.

What we did do, however, was pray. Together, the fearful people of Jerusalem, people of all faiths, the Fatamid defenders, and the Seljuks joined together for one final display of our faith. It was our last cry for help, our last gasp, our last chance to reach out to God with our thoughts and ask Him to save us.

Soon, it would be time to defend Jerusalem, and we needed whatever light we could pull into our souls, for what was coming was a shadow of hell itself.

As the sun disappeared and darkness fell on the holy city, the mighty army of Raymond rumbled towards us. Overhead, the clouds occasionally blocked the starlight, which left my view of the thousands of invaders fading in and out of darkness.

Battle cries echoed out from Jerusalem, and from the soldiers who barreled towards us. I glanced back to the city. Terrified people, mostly elderly and women, huddled up and prayed. Parents held their children close.

Jerusalem's defenders let loose a wave of arrows and felled a group of infantry. I took aim along with Zahra, and we fired our own shots. I hit someone in the chest. He dropped to the ground in a heap. I grimaced, but I nocked my next arrow.

Zahra nailed two targets of her own, and she remained steady. Meanwhile, the brotherhood regrouped and added their bows to ours. But Raymond's forces persisted. Their numbers allowed them to get right up to the walls.

From somewhere behind me, I heard someone call out, "The knights have broken in on the other side! We have to get to the keep!"

No! I thought. They already breached the defenses? I had no time to think. They were about to do the same here.

Two siege towers collided into the walls, and dozens of ladders were planted from below. We were simply too few to defend against this army. Men piled onto the walls from the towers, and armored heads popped up from the ladders. We were quickly overwhelmed. I fought with Zahra behind me and the brotherhood beside me. We deflected the blows of the rage-filled soldiers of God. It was a wave of ferocious zeal that was set to wash us all away.

The brotherhood began to fall. Nine were cut down in a blur of steel and anger, and finally Naasir had a sword run through his gut.

I fought off a few soldiers, but I lost energy quickly. Hilal preserved my life more than once as I fought back the invaders' angry, vicious strikes. Just when there seemed to be a break in the numbers, a familiar figure jumped from the siege tower: Raymond.

He killed several of Jerusalem's defenders with ease, and his armor was spattered with their blood. When he saw me, his expression turned even fiercer. He ran towards me and called off the men who attacked.

Immediately, he tried to kill me. He swung his sword down in rage, and it cracked into my shield. I deflected the blow – barely – and slashed him in the leg, which did nothing because of his armor. He kicked my shield away and tried to lop off my head with his next strike. Zahra shrieked as I narrowly escaped death a second time. Raymond moved so quickly despite his age – despite the horrors he'd seen, endured, and inflicted – and he lashed out quickly with a sword slash that streaked across my cheek. As the blood ran down my face, Raymond punched me, and I crashed into the stone wall. I struggled to my feet.

Raymond watched as Zahra, Hilal, and I were backed into a corner. Knights streamed up the ladders behind him and poured into the city. Then my mentor smiled slightly – enough for us to know that he had us beaten.

"This journey has been a nightmare," he grimly said as his smile dipped. "So I'm going to have a little fun. Julien – I dare you to survive. I dare you to find me and prove to me that your twisted beliefs are worth a damn."

"I owe you nothing," I shouted. "Nothing but a quick death – and that's more than you deserve."

"How loving of you, my boy." He scoffed. "I might say the same of you." He pointed his crimson blade at me. "Go on, Julien. Fight. Struggle. And see how long you and that fool girl survive. If you make it to me – I will have a gift for you."

The cruel luxury I had been extended wasn't offered to the brotherhood. I could only watch on, weakened, as the rest of the brotherhood was overwhelmed and executed. Hilal fought valiantly, but he was the last to be slain. Those brave soldiers who had stood with me were all silenced. It crushed my soul and left me in desperate tears. I had been powerless to help my friends. Raymond's offer to live was a miserable, heinous prize. Truthfully, if it wasn't for Zahra's sake, I don't think I would've accepted it. I would've fought to the death right there and then.

Raymond and his forces moved on, washing into the city like a poisonous wave. I strained a few steps to the edge of the stone wall and saw the city streets below. Everyone inside was being slaughtered. I asked Zahra to turn away, but she couldn't. The terrified screams and wails were from the darkest nightmares, and the blood coated the streets in red. The faithful wiped out the Fatimid soldiers, and they smashed their way into homes – women and children were dragged out and cut down just the same. This can't be, I thought. Many of these people are Christians… their crosses are plain to see! How can they do this? Even the churches and mosques were not exempt from this massacre. Bodies quickly piled up outside their doors.

As the screams grew fainter, and the army pushed inwards, Zahra helped me up to my feet. I was wobbly, and Zahra patched me up with some bandages. Her hands shook as she removed a bloody cloth from my face.

"I think you're okay," she said, her voice tinged with fear. "You'll be okay, right?"

"I'm okay... Thank you, Zahra. How... how has this happened?"

"I don't know. But we'll get through it, right?"

I nodded slowly. "Right."

Another few men came up the ladders and burst by us in frenzy. One stopped. He was interested in Zahra. I found what strength I could – I knocked him away – but I don't know if I could've bested him in my exhaustion. He rushed in to go for Zahra, but she stabbed him right in the neck with the dagger Ahtmar had insisted she wear. The soldier crumbled and bled out on the stone below.

Zahra's crimson-soaked hands trembled. She never deserved this. She was an angel among demons.

"Ahtmar..." she quietly said. "In the end, you saved me again. Thank you..." She broke down in tears. I said a prayer for Ahtmar, who had watched over his sister – even from the heavens.

We pushed into the city. Somehow, we had to make it back to the front gates, but heaven called to me – I couldn't walk away while Raymond stained the holy city with the blood of the innocent. I battled my weakness and self-doubt and pushed away crippling exhaustion with pure, nauseating willpower, but I found it within myself to think: with you, God, all things are possible. Please – give me the strength to show my mentor how wrong he is.

The streets were littered with the broken bodies of men,

women, and children. We had to step over stray limbs, and my boots were colored red. Nearby, my former allies claimed prizes as they robbed homes. Coin purses and gold jewelry jingled alongside the cries of slaughter.

We made it to a cross street. The Christian quarter was in one direction, and it was not spared either. Angry warriors streamed through the gates, and they carried a frightful killing intent with their blades drawn.

While Zahra and I did our best to keep hidden, the violence had been so vicious and blinding that I wonder if it masked our presence. The knights seemed to be in a bloodlust dream.

We walked for a while and avoided more bodies until we came to another religious center. There was a church and a mosque opposite one another. Both doors were closed and locked tightly. I saw the terrified faces of citizens as they watched from the windows. Down one of the streets, a collection of knights headed our way. They were led by Raymond and Tancred. They stopped in the courtyard, and my former mentor scattered his forces in different directions. He asked Tancred to go and claim one of the temples, and then Raymond approached me alone.

"So here we are," he muttered. "You made it."

"I want you to know something," I firmly said. "I did not come here because of your offer – your 'gift.' I came here to show you how utterly wrong you are – how that nightmare journey you spoke of was all caused by you. You and your army. Your blind beliefs."

"Faith is blind," the knight confidently said. "It always has been, and always will be. But look around you. We may not see God, but He sees us."

I shook my head, utterly without words at such a dark thought.

"You know something," Raymond continued. "Adhemar had a

234

dying wish." My heart sunk as I realized the bishop had fallen. My mentor pointed at Zahra, and I moved in front of her. His silver hand slowly dropped. "It was to preserve her – and you."

I raised my head. "Why?"

"He saw something in you. He said you were destined to do something great, one day. And he said the girl you saved should be saved a second time. He thought it was destiny, or some such absurdity. In his death throes, he saw mad visions."

"We don't need your pity," Zahra said bitterly, in Latin. "We need you to disappear from this world."

Raymond shook his head. "I have more to do."

"As do I," I said.

"Well, in any case, I thought – to honor bishop Adhemar – I would meet him halfway. I would give you a chance, Julien." He lifted his finger. "One more chance."

"I would never accept anything from you, ever again," I barked.

A group of knights streamed in front one of the streets. They carried their stolen riches and the marks of their bloody deeds across their armor. They surrounded us.

"Reconsider," Raymond said.

Zahra moved behind me. "What the hell do you want from me?" I asked my mentor.

"Face me in a duel." My mentor paced back and forth. "Fight me. If you lose, you die."

"And when I win?" I shouted.

"If you win, then you live. You can walk away."

"And how do I know you'll honor the terms? How do I know you won't simply cut me down?"

"You hurt me, Julien," Raymond said as he narrowed his eyes. "The truth is, you don't know. But I am an honorable man, and I will honor the deal. These men will bear witness."

The group of crimson-spattered knights cheered.

"Don't do it, Julien," Zahra whispered. "Don't give him what he wants."

"The truth is," I whispered back, "this isn't just what he wants. It's wrong, but... I want it too."

With that, I stepped forward and pointed my blade at the man who, for so long, defined me.

The knights made a circle, a man-made, sickening coliseum to honor our foolish duel. But as far as I knew, this was our only way out. I had told Zahra I'd wanted this, too, and as much as I did, I realized how impossible it was to convince a monster like Raymond that he was wrong.

But I'd done the impossible before – I'd allied with the Turks, made them my dearest friends, and fallen in love with Zahra. If anything, the impossible was within my grasp.

Raymond gave me no time to ponder. He quickly lunged ahead, screamed, and swung his blade right at my skull. I weaved to the side and slashed him in the chest, but his chainmail protected him well. We slammed into each other with our fists, and his hurt me much more than I hurt him. I collapsed.

I scrambled to my feet, and my vision was a hazy blur. In the distance, the knights looked like monstrous shadows. Behind them, faint figures ran for their lives.

I ducked Raymond's next strike too slowly. He battered my shoulder with his blade, which sent me back to the ground. Zahra cried out, and her voice lent me the strength to stand.

"Give up," Raymond barked. "Everything we've done was right, and true, and just. Say it, and I might let you live. Say it."

"Never," I cried as I raged ahead. I crashed right into my mentor and knocked him back a few steps. He twisted his body and hurled me back to the dirt. I screamed in bloody rage and charged at him again. He tripped me, and then slammed a boot into my back. I tumbled down.

Even though I was exhausted, and I nearly choked on dirt and sand, I realized something. Ironically, it was something I'd learned from Raymond. Fighting angry wouldn't work. I had to be calm. My mind spun, between the blows I'd been dealt, the screams of the innocent in the distance, and the weight of my love's life – I had to have faith that there was a way through this darkness.

I strained to push up onto my knees and peered up at Raymond, who wore pure confidence on his face. I coughed up some dirt, and then sucked in a new breath of air – I imagined it being light and hope. I pulled sparking energy into the kingdom of heaven within me. And I exhaled fear. I pictured it being a bitter yellow energy that God took from me and sent into the dark skies above.

I pulled up my sword and shield, which was cracked and almost broken. This time, I waited for Raymond.

He smiled, I think. And then he charged, using precise, powerful swings to try and break through my guard. I used what I'd learned from him. I angled my body slightly to lessen his blows, and then, just as he swung as hard as he could, I slammed into him and tackled him to the ground.

I mounted him and bashed his head with my sword hilt. Over and over, I attacked, and it was a dire struggle not to strike in murderous rage. Instead, I held that light inside of me – Zahra's light, and God's light, and tried to show him that I'd won. He wouldn't accept it.

I aimed a final punch for his jaw, and he quickly moved his

head. I struck the ground and screamed in pain. Raymond threw all of his weight up, and I was thrown off of him. We both fought back to our feet.

For the first time, Raymond took in heavy breaths. He stared at me hatefully, and probably wondered where I'd found my strength.

He raced towards me, and now, his swings were inelegant and wild. I dodged them easily, and then I bashed him in the face with my shield, which rocked him. He swung again, and his blade got trapped in my splintered shield. He pulled it from me with all of his strength and sent the shield flying out of reach. It had become sword versus sword.

We paced around each other, and my mind was dull from the screams of the battle-hungry demons around us. I tried to block all of the noise and focus only on my mentor. He was bleeding from somewhere on his head, and his eyes looked heavy.

"Come on, Julien," he shouted. "What are you waiting for?"

I didn't listen. I saw through the trap, and instead remained defensive. My mentor blinked quickly and looked more and more unsteady. Finally, he raised his shoulders, and made one last attack.

He moved like lightning and swung his sword down from above. He tried to split me in two. But I blocked him with my blade – I held all of his weight, his power, his anger, his dreadful hatred, and I let him stay there. I let him struggle and realize he couldn't win. And then, he fell.

His body had gone limp, and he actually toppled right into me, which took me with him to the ground. I struggled to get free with the weight of his armor, and eventually I squirmed away.

The knights were not pleased. They moved in closer to us. They threatened us and cursed at us. It looked like all was lost, like we'd never see a new day, but then, Raymond woke up.

"Stop," he cried, his words weak and unsteady. "Stop it right now." The bloody knights stumbled back like children caught doing something they shouldn't.

Raymond pushed onto an elbow, then a knee, and remained there. He looked at me, and grinned. "You win, Julien." Before I spoke, he said, "Get out of here. Go live your fucking life."

I shakily said, "And what will you do? Will you burn down these holy places – will you continue this senseless slaughter?"

My mentor stared at me coldly. The sad truth was, I couldn't convince him of anything.

"No one could have stopped what happened here today, Julien. No one. This was a divine plan."

"You're wrong," I barked. My mentor was unfazed.

Raymond rubbed his jaw and managed a chuckle. "You really got me good there." He sighed. "You know… if there was something that got in the way, it was you, my boy. You are a wrinkle in God's vision."

"You might call me an exception," I firmly said, "but I am the example. And Raymond – I will see to it that this can never happen again. I will carry the news of this day to the world, and I will forge a new peace between the faiths."

"Well, that's noble." Raymond managed to get back to his feet. He shoved away the knights who tried to help him. "I wish you the best, despite everything."

I swallowed hard. I couldn't say the same thing to him.

I wondered if I should I have tried to take Raymond down. If I should have fought on valiantly like the brotherhood, who gave their lives to protect Jerusalem. When I looked at Zahra, her terrified face gave my answer. That message echoed in my mind again: there is more to do. I'd thought it was about Jerusalem, but maybe it was about something further in the future.

Zahra and I walked by Raymond and Tancred, towards the gates I had previously guarded. I slowed down and turned back.

"Raymond... sir. I thank you for giving us this chance." Despite my anger, despite my heartache, I meant it.

"Yes," he replied. "Just take advantage of it while you can. I can't guarantee that some knights won't go chasing after you for the things you've done... Someday, maybe we'll meet again. Goodbye, Julien."

We eventually made it through the gates, out into the sand. Ahtmar's body was before us, buried by arrows. Zahra broke down and fell to her knees. I knew there was nothing to say. Instead, I knelt beside her and prayed. It only made her cry harder, but I hoped that one day soon I could dry her eyes.

I waited, I shared in her tears, and I mourned with her, until she was ready.

If there was one miracle that had occurred, it was that Jisra had survived – my horse was outside the walls. She dug her hooves into the ground like nothing was wrong.

"Jisra!" I called. Zahra and I ran over together. "You made it, girl!"

We both fawned over her like we'd found a rare treasure. With that, our energy slowly returned to us.

"Julien, what do you think we should do?"

"We have to get far away from here." I peered towards the night sky, the stars and the moon. Somehow, I felt a swell of positive energy. "After that... well, there's a big world out there. And as long as I'm with you, I'm happy to explore it."

"Yes... What you said before – I want to follow that dream, Julien. I want to carry the news of what happened here across the world. I want to create a time where this will never happen again."

"That's exactly what I was thinking."

Jerusalem had changed me forever. I would carry the souls of the dead with me wherever I go. They are part of me. They weigh me down and haunt my dreams. But there was another side to it – I would carry the knowledge to pass on to a new generation, so that we might learn from our mistakes.

With that resolution firmly in my mind, I said, "Let's change the world, Zahra."

We galloped ahead on a new path, towards the unknown. We left the horror of Jerusalem behind, and though it would always be a deep wound of my past, I wanted to focus on the future. With an angel like Zahra by my side, anything seemed possible. We would bring those dreams to life.

———————

Several Months Later

Zahra and I had brought the news of the siege of Jerusalem through Egypt. We saw the stunning pyramids, the relics of another great civilization, and we carried the truth onward from there.

Despite Raymond's offer to let us go, some of his knights had set out to kill us. Whether they were under his order or not – I'm not certain.

We left over twenty of them dead. I had told myself that I would protect the love that Zahra and I share – and I would make sure the truth was heard.

I trained Zahra using what I'd learned. Her muscles were bigger, and she stood tall and proud. She was always strong, but she would be able to topple any knight with a sword as well as her wonderful heart.

We didn't know what the future held, but our journey continued. We planned to see new lands together, to bring forth a peaceful era, and my deepest prayer remained – I wanted our love to change this world forever.

Printed in the USA
CPSIA information can be obtained
at www.ICGtesting.com
LVHW051130050724
784393LV00009B/18

9 781953 971975